I W DO ANYTHING FOR LOVE

NEW LOVERS is a series devoted to
publishing new works of erotica
that explore the complexities
bedevilling contemporary
life, culture, and
art today.

I WOULD DO ANYTHING FOR LOVE

×

AL BEDELL

BADLANDS UNLIMITED
NEW LOVERS
Nº5

I Would Do Anything For Love
by Al Bedell

New Lovers No.5

Published by:
Badlands Unlimited LLC
P.O. Box 320310
Brooklyn, NY 11232
Tel: +1 718 788 6668
operator@badlandsunlimited.com
www.badlandsunlimited.com

Series editors: Paul Chan, Ian Cheng, Micaela Durand, Matthew So
Copy editor: Charlotte Carter
Editorial assistant: Jessica Jackson
Ebook designer: Ian Cheng
Front cover design by Kobi Benzari
Special thanks to Angela Brown, Luke Brown, Martha Fleming-Ives, Elisa
Leshowitz, Marlo Poras

Paper book distributed in the Americas by:
ARTBOOK | D.A.P. USA
155 6th Avenue, 2nd Floor
New York, NY 10013
Tel. +1 800 338 BOOK
www.artbook.com

Paper book distributed in Europe by:
Buchhandlung Walther König
Ehrenstrasse 4
50672 Köln
www.buchhandlung-walther-koenig.de

Printed in the United States of America

ISBN: 978-1-936440-93-1
E-Book ISBN: 978-1-936440-94-8

www.badlandsunlimited.com

CONTENTS

Mike A

Princess Cecily shivers as she waits for her royal carriage. Shrill chanting haunts the air as fiery fairies perform their nightly virgin sacrifice. The Princess has never been fond of this eon-old ritual, but even though she is a princess, there are many things out of her control. Her father, the King, is an orthodox ruler and a firm believer in upholding tradition. Her long peach gown is made of silk thin enough to show every curve of her slender frame. It flows to her ankles and kisses her dainty feet. Her back is exposed to the cool spring air. Long golden locks cascade from the tiara perched on her head. She covers her ears and shivers again. It's chilly for March.

Princess Cecily sighs with relief as her Pegasus-drawn carriage appears through the pink mist. The vibrant magenta fur of the winged steeds glitters under a tie-dye sky. The cream and gold carriage illuminates the purple flowers that line the cobblestone path. The Princess grins as a large brown bear brings the carriage to a halt. "Sorry to keep you waiting, Princess." The coachbear ties the Pegasus reigns to a post. "Lots of sky traffic this evening."

"It is quite all right, Cocoa. I know I can always count on you."

Cocoa Bear hugs the princess and wipes a tear from his furry face. "You're growing up too fast, Princess. It seems like just yesterday you were running around the garden in nothing but your royal diaper."

"Please do not bring that up again, Cocoa. I'm fifteen years old and to be wed soon."

"My apologies, Your Highness."

To Princess Cecily's shock the carriage door opens from the inside.

"Mike A!" Cecily shrieks. "What are you doing in there? If my father knew of this, he would offer me to the fiery fairies in a heartbeat."

Mike A chuckles as he pulls the princess into the carriage. He wears a dapper tuxedo with a red rose pinned to the lapel and his sapphire eyes gleam in the moonlight. Tousled brown hair brushes his perfect forehead. "I needed to see you even for a few moments." He smiles at his fair maiden. Unable to hide her excitement, Cecily tackles Mike A with a series of playful kisses.

Still holding the carriage door open for the young lovers, the royal coachbear clears his throat. Princess Cecily peels herself from Mike A and turns to her old friend. "Mum's the word, Bear."

"As you wish, Princess." Cocoa nods his large head with mischievous understanding. "To be a young cub again," he says, laughing. "To the castle?"

"Yes, of course," Princess Cecily responds as the royal coachbear gently closes the carriage door. "I need to be home by 10 P.M., as always."

"Your wish is my command." The coachbear mounts the front of the carriage and whips the two winged stallions, cueing them to canter into the night sky.

"You're crazy, Mike A—absolutely mad." Princess Cecily squeezes Mike A. "But I'm glad you're here."

"Perhaps I am crazy, my Princess." Mike A kisses Princess Cecily on the cheek. "But I am not at fault. You drive me wild! Watching you dance with all of those unworthy men was sheer torture. I could barely see straight. All I could think about was holding your body against mine and fucking your royal brains out."

"Mike A!" Princess Cecily shouts and nudges him with her elbow. "I'm so dizzy from all of that waltzing!" She shimmies closer to her charming companion and smiles. "And you know that as a princess it is my duty to dance with any man who asserts the waltz with me." The Princess looks down at her lap. "Even if I don't like them."

"A despicable convention!" Mike A barks. "A girl of your age should be able to choose who she will and will not dance with!"

Princess Cecily grazes Mike A's face with her delicate hand and frowns. "It's just how it's always been."

"I know, but that doesn't make it right."

"There's no use wasting our precious time

together discussing things neither of us has the power to change," Cecily snaps. "Let's talk about something else."

Mike A kisses her sweetly. "Sure, let's talk about little Princess Cecily running through the garden in nothing but her diaper! What I wouldn't do to see that!"

"Mike A!" Cecily's cheeks rapidly turn a rosy shade of embarrassment. "I ought to bring that coachbear to the royal taxidermist."

Mike A laughs. "I bet you were a cute baby!"

"Obviously," Princess Cecily responds, "but I am a woman now," she rubs Mike A's thigh, "and I have womanly desires." She nibbles his ear and moves her hand over his growing bulge. "And I wouldn't mind seeing you stark naked in the garden either."

"Oh, Princess…" Mike A recoils. "I…"

Princess Cecily looks at the orange moon. "It's almost ten." She climbs onto Mike A's lap and straddles him. "We don't have much time!" Feverishly removing Mike A's jacket, Princess Cecily stares deep into Mike A's eyes. "Take me."

Mike A adjusts his hips and crawls on top of the Princess as she wraps her long legs around his muscular torso. Urging him closer, she nibbles his earlobe and squeezes his back. Mike's A.'s trembling breath runs down Cecily's neck, down to her ribs and finally her groin. She pulsates when she feels Mike A's rapidly growing bulge between her thighs. Pulling the soft gown up to her waist, he pushes her lace panties to the side and rubs her tenderly. As he caresses Cecily below, Mike A sticks two fingers into Cecily's mouth. Wet and eager with desire, Princess Cecily unzips his trousers and gazes upon his dripping erection. She then looks into Mike A's befuddled eyes and kisses him passionately. In a swift maneuver he lays his Princess across the seat, cupping the back of her head with care. Cecily wraps her legs and arms around her prince and they melt into each other as if their shared breaths are keeping one another alive. She pushes her panties further to the side and inserts her noble prince with slippery ease. The royal lovers sigh in unison as he plunges into Cecily slowly and deeply. As he rhythmically thrusts into his fair princess, both are completely engulfed in passion. She digs her pink nails into Mike A's shoulders as he drives even deeper.

As the young lovers escalate with fervor the carriage lands on the ground with a hard thud.

"Ten! Ten! Ten! It's almost ten!" Cecily shouts with delight and takes Mike A deeper.

"Oh, Princess," Mike A huffs. "I'm almost there!" The horses' hooves clomp down the cobblestones, shaking the carriage for a welcomed commotion. The carriage rocks at the same pace as their heavy panting and the tiara falls from Cecily's royal head. Filled to the brim with sheer bliss, Princess Cecily convulses and kicks her leg through the window with uninhibited pleasure. "This is going to be the best Spring Break ever!"

Cecily wakes up in her twin bed at her mother's house on the first morning of Spring Break. Her mother is not a queen and Cecily has never worn a pair of stilettos in her life. There is nothing extraordinary about Cecily Scott. The furthest she's ever been from her rural hometown in Pennsylvania is Ft. Lauderdale, Florida, when she was six years old, and the only thing she remembers is being too afraid to swim in her aunt's pool. While her cousins swam, Cecily would sprawl out on the floor in the dining room. She preferred the relief of cold tiles on her body in the hot, sticky Florida climate.

Wearing sweatpants and a bleach-stained

purple t-shirt, Cecily rolls out of bed and walks outside to get the mail, as she does every day. She knows there is nothing there for her.

Heading back inside, Cecily moseys over to the kitchen. She opens the fridge and picks at some of last night's leftovers with her fingers. Cold macaroni and cheese. She heats up some of the neon yellow elbow pasta in the microwave and takes it to the living room, turns on the TV. *"Find out what happens when people stop being polite and start getting real.* The Real World, Seattle."

"Cec, honey, chicken cutlets for dinner." Cecily's mother shakes her from the couch. "Sound good? How's Spring Break? You de-stressing? You haven't been sitting in front of the TV all day, have you? Work was crazy. I showed the house on Cedar Street to the Johnsons again. I think they're going to make an offer. They love the foyer, the in-ground swimming pool, and it's in the best school district in the county." TV murmurs the Final Jeopardy theme song.

The next day, Cecily eats cold chicken cutlets for breakfast, lunch, and dinner. She wakes up when her mother tells her they'll be having hot dogs that night. Tacos tomorrow. Now lodged into Cecily's head, the theme song to *The Price is Right* haunts the unkempt house.

"Your mom's cooking skills are improving! She used wheels instead of elbows this time!" Cecily's best friend Liz swallows a heaping spoonful of macaroni and cheese.

"I hate macaroni and cheese," Cecily grumbles. "I want to dye my hair blonde."

"Cec, your hair is jet black, it will never take." Cecily forcefully drags Liz into the bathroom. "I don't care. We're doing this." *Wheel of Fortune* plays from the living room.

"Cecily Nicole Scott, what on Earth have you done to your hair?" Cecily's mother shrieks.

"That is incorrect. The question is 'What is the World's Fair?'" Alex Trebek condescends.

"It's my summer look, Mom. I'm fifteen and I want to have fun! Everyone knows blondes have more fun."

"You look like your aunt Beth after her second divorce."

Cecily pouts and combs her fingers through her brittle copper-colored hair.

"I'm sorry, sweetie. I've had a long day and the traffic was terrible on the way home." Cecily's mother touches her daughter's hair and smiles. "It's not all that bad. Change is a good thing, right?" She hugs her daughter tight. "You're beautiful, Cecily Scott. I love you so much. You're my pride and joy. I've given up my entire life for you, and I'd do it again in a heartbeat." She lets go of Cecily and retreats to the kitchen. "Hamburger Helper tonight."

"Love you too, Mom."

"Everyone's going to The Diner tonight. It's tradition," Cecily explains. "On the last night of Spring Break, all of the Brax Boys go to the town diner and then party in the parking lot. We have to go!"

Liz flips through a magazine on Cecily's bedroom floor and points to a picture of a famous blonde woman in the magazine. "You can probably get your hair to this color after two more processes." She turns the page. "And I don't think you look like your aunt Beth. You have all your teeth."

Cecily looks at the mirror, analyzing her face framed by her newly damaged hair. Her eyebrows have never looked so bushy; her cheeks have never seemed so puffy. Her jaw definition is a thing of the past. She touches her stomach. *No more mac and cheese*, she thinks.

"It's not like anyone is going to talk to us, Cecily." Liz pours a bag of Skittles into her mouth. "But I'm up for it. Will your mom be able to drive us?"

"Yeah, she'll drive us," Cecily responds. "Do you think Mike A will be there?" She walks to her dresser. "I hate all of my clothes. I don't know what to wear in March. It's sunny but still cold and I can't show my legs. They're so pale. I don't even have a light jacket. Are windbreakers lame?" Growing frantic, Cecily throws her cousin's old windbreaker across the room. "Do you think Mike A likes blondes? He probably thinks windbreakers are lame."

"Windbreakers are lame," Liz assures her overwrought friend. "And you look great, Cec. You always do. Just wear a hoodie." Liz throws the magazine in the waste bin.

"I'll have a cheeseburger—well done—a side of fries, and a Coke," Liz orders.

"I'll just have salad." Cecily hands the menu to the waitress. "With Ranch dressing," she adds as she puts her hood up. Attempting to achieve invisibility, Cecily sinks into the booth and looks around the small town diner as it pulses with excitement, tension, and uncertainty. Everyone from West Braxton High is there. She is not hungry.

There he is. Mike A, flawless as can be, struts in with the rest of the most popular boys at West Braxton High. They call themselves the Brax Boys and they always travel in a pack. Mike A wears a cream colored polo with blue stripes and acid wash jeans. His Reeboks are gray, formerly white. He sports the signature blue and gold letterman jacket that all the Brax Boys wear. To the untrained eye it is nearly impossible to tell the Brax Boys apart but Cecily can spot her Mike A from light years away. His blue eyes shoot warm lasers through her entire body and soul. She is paralyzed by his pure perfection. Accompanied by a handful of the most popular girls in school, the Brax Boys storm the largest booth in the diner. "We want everything!" a Brax Boy demands. Mike A disappears amongst the commotion of his pack chanting "SPRING BREAK! SPRING BREAK! SPRING BREAK!" As waitresses scramble to seat the disruptive patrons, Cecily focuses on chipping the beet colored polish off her nails so as not to gawk at the man of her dreams. Liz finishes her first glass of Coke.

"Oh my god, Liz. He's here. Oh my god." Cecily panics and pulls her hood lower onto her face. "What should I do? This was a mistake. Just the sight of him makes me feel faint. How am I ever going to talk to him? We should have just stayed home and watched that TV movie my mom wouldn't shut up about. This is bad, Liz. I can't believe he's here."

Liz slowly turns away from the plate of nachos she has been ogling. "Who's here?" She props herself up in the booth to get a better view.

"Mike A!" Cecily snaps under her breath. "Sit down!"

"Cec, relax. We knew the Brax Boys would be here, remember?" Liz places a napkin on her lap. "Let's just be cool, okay? We're freshmen— it'd be a miracle if a Brax Boy would grant us the honor of washing his dishes." She looks around the diner again. "Where is our food? I know they're busy, but I'm starving!"

A frosted plastic plate of iceberg lettuce, sliced pale tomato, and soggy cucumber is placed in front of Cecily and she stares at her side of Ranch dressing. *Ew*, she thinks. "I have to go wash my hands," she says, shifting her gaze from the nauseating food to her mutilated fingernails.

"Okay, but hurry up! Your delicious meal might get cold!" Liz chuckles and dips a fry into ketchup. Cecily ignores her friend's signature sarcasm and slides from the booth, shivering because her legs are freezing. Liz takes a satisfying bite of the luscious burger. "Oh yeah, and if you see our waitress can you ask her for another Coke?" Cecily disregards this request and flees the table.

Cecily sneaks past the Brax Boys with her hands in her pockets. Peeking out of her hood she glances toward the chaos, hoping by some miracle she will lock eyes with Mike A. However, senior Brax Boys are too busy chanting "CLASS OF '95! CLASS OF '95!" to notice the hooded freshman girl with pale legs walk by.

Cecily pokes at her pathetic salad with a fork as Liz finishes her burger. "I feel bad for the waitresses here," Liz says. "This place is a madhouse."

"They're used to it," Cecily says. "It's tradition." She covers her full plate with a napkin and wishes she had ordered a burger.

"Oh my god, Cecily," Liz whispers. "Don't freak out."

"About what?"

"Don't look, but Mike A is walking over here," Liz whispers with a mouth full of potato. Cecily swirls the ice cubes around in her glass of water. "Oh my god."

"You girls wanna hang?"

Cecily looks up from her ice cubes and convinces herself she is dreaming. Mike A is standing in front of her booth speaking actual words to her. His voice washes over her, rendering her speechless. Goosebumps trickle from her arms to her legs. There is no way this is happening.

"You mean in the parking lot?" Liz asks Mike A, rescuing Cecily from her lustful stupor.

"Yeah." Mike A sticks his hands in his pockets and catches eyes with one of the Brax Boys. He turns back to the freshman girls. "The parking lot."

"Sure, we just need to get the check. We'll see you there," Cecily somehow responds, though she doesn't recognize her own voice. She pinches her knee to make sure everything's real.

"Cool. Oh, and tip well. These poor waitresses have been through a lot tonight. See you in the lot, Cecily." Mike A walks out of the diner.

"Liz, am I hallucinating or did Mike A say my name?"

"He said your name, Cec. I know. I'm freaking out too. Let's just take deep breaths and act natural."

"Act natural," Cecily sighs.

"Yeah, act natural," Liz repeats.

"Here goes nothing."

Fifteen cars are parked in the lot behind the diner, hidden from the street. "Carry On, Wayward Son" blares from a Volvo. Thirty or forty people gather around a Jeep as a Brax Boy hands everyone Styrofoam cups of Bud Light. Cecily and Liz follow along and thank the Brax Boy for their beverages. Neither girl has ever consumed alcohol before.

"Cheers!" they say in unison, tapping their cups together. "Act natural, it's just beer," utters Liz.

Cecily grimaces. "This is disgusting. It's warm." They sip slowly.

Cecily notices Hazel, a petite blonde senior wearing shorts and a red Cornell sweatshirt. Hazel stumbles around with a cup in each hand and a lit cigarette hangs from her glossy pink lips. The red bow in her hair is perfectly lopsided. "Where's the grass?!" Hazel slurs as she tumbles onto the lap of a red haired Brax Boy. Hazel presses her lips to his and inhales as the Brax Boy exhales smoke into her lungs. She drops both cups on the ground and they kiss feverishly. Moments later, they're in the back of a Honda Civic.

Sipping from her cup, Cecily observes many of her peers coupling off into cars. A Ford Taurus bumps up and down.

"She's wasted," Liz mutters.

"I heard she's always wasted." Cecily surveys the parking lot crowd. "Is that Isabel over there?"

"Yeah, I think it is," Liz confirms. "She seems happy."

"I guess so." Suddenly a Brax Boy stumbles into Cecily, nearly knocking her over. Her beer spills all over her bare legs.

"Easy there, freshman. Is this your first rodeo?"

"Kind of, yeah," Cecily responds, but the Brax Boy is now taking part in another SPRING BREAK chant.

"I can't believe we're here, Liz." Cecily grins. "This is incredible. I'm going to get another cup of beer. Do you want one?"

"No, I'm still working on mine." Liz sips

again. "It's still disgusting. And warm." Cecily walks to the beer Jeep and the prince of her dreams appears before her at the keg. "Act natural," she says to herself.

"It's Cecily, right?" Mike A pumps the keg and pierces Cecily with his captivating blue eyes.

"That's correct," Cecily answers. "Cecily Scott."

"Here you go, Cecily Scott." Mike A extends his manly arm to Cecily, offering her another cup of vile beer. "Getting wild tonight?" He grins. Dimples take over his gorgeous face.

"Thanks." Cecily takes the beer from Mike A's hands. For a brief moment their fingers touch and Cecily retracts her hand. "I mean, I don't really drink much and my mom is picking me up at ten."

"Wow. Ten. Cinderella at least had until midnight."

"Well, she wasn't thrilled about letting me out on a school night in the first place, but I told her it was a West Braxton tradition. She supports traditions, I suppose." Cecily looks at the ground as she tries to comprehend what just spilled out of her mouth. *I suppose?*

"Your mom is right. It's important to uphold traditions. It gives people a sense of security, even if it's false and fleeting. Something to look forward to, you know?" Cecily nods in agreement. "It's like, regardless of any shitty curve balls the universe throws at you—whether you flunked a math test, or your dad walked out on you for a new family and refuses to answer your phone calls, or if you don't get into your dream school on the west coast—not that you could afford tuition anyway—all of that stuff is unpredictable. If you have this event, this tradition, at least you have something constant. It's not going to change. Every year, I know what to expect from the Lot party. We booze, we get high, blast music, and makes fools of ourselves.

We can forget about all of the stuff that we can't control for a little while."

"Yeah," Cecily responds. "That's pretty much what I told my mom."

"You know what, Cecily Scott? I wasn't expecting one thing to happen tonight. It's happening right now."

"What's happening?"

"The prettiest girl in the student body is standing in front of me, and I'm gushing about my pathetic life."

"I'm not the prettiest." Cecily nearly chokes on her beer. "And I don't think you're pathetic."

"Thank you, Cecily Scott, but you have no idea." Mike A chugs his Bud Light and fills another cup to the brim. Cecily sips slowly, still not used to the taste. "You want to get in this car?" Mike A taps on the car he is leaning against.

"Right now?" Cecily is overwhelmed with

excitement. This is real life, not a dream. She tugs on her hair to confirm. "With you?"

"Unless you have someone else in mind." Mike A smiles.

"Sure, but I only have a few minutes before my mom gets here."

"I know, I know, or you'll turn into a pumpkin."

Cecily scans the lot and spots Liz chatting with some Brax Boys and a few girls from her swim team.

"After you, m'lady." Mike A opens the door to a Ford Focus and Cecily slides in. Mike A follows.

"Yeah, I like tradition too. I wish Spring Break lasted longer," Cecily says.

"Too much freedom is dangerous, Cecily Scott. Trust me."

Mike A positions his body so his knee jabs into the side of Cecily's thigh, but she doesn't mind. She tries to take deep breaths and act natural, but it's as if she's forgotten how to breathe altogether. She glances at Mike A, giggles, and twirls the drawstring on her hoodie.

Mike A touches Cecily's strawlike hair, gently moving his hand to the back of her neck. His index finger navigates her earlobe. Cecily remembers how to breathe and she's breathing heavily and trembling slightly. Mike A leans over and softly kisses her neck. She shivers even though she's not cold anymore.

Mike A's hands are under Cecily's hoodie as she wraps her arms around his neck, holding him tighter, kissing him deeper. Desperate for more, she takes her hoodie off.

"Hey, let's slow down. You don't want to do anything you're going to regret," Mike A says.

"I want to do this. I want you," Cecily coos.

Mike A looks at his watch. "Wow, Cecily. Your mom is going to be here any minute."

"Oh god. You're right!" Cecily quickly dresses and attempts to smooth her hair. She darts out of the car. "Well, see you at school tomorrow!" Cecily squeaks.

"Count on it." Mike A pours out the rest of his beer. "And hey, thanks for making this parking lot feel like Camelot, Princess Cecily."

"Likewise!" Ordinary Cecily Scott would be well aware that his line is corny, but Princess Cecily's heart melts.

Peeling Liz from the arms of a tall, tan Brax Boy, the two ordinary freshman girls run to Cecily's mother's minivan in the front of the diner. Ten on the dot.

"Did you have fun, girls?" Cecily's mother asks from the front seat.

"Yeah, but not *too* much fun," Cecily responds. "It's a school night, after all." Cecily's mother starts the engine. "Good girl," she says.

"This has been the best Spring Break ever!" Liz shouts as Cecily buckles her seatbelt for her.

"The burgers here are delicious, Mom. You have got to try them sometime."

Mike B

"He knows," Cecily says as she flails her hands in front of her, attempting to dry her wet nail polish. A magazine falls off the bed and displays an ad for eyeshadow.

"Who knows what?" Liz scours her bag of gummy bears, looking for a red one. She pops an orange gummy bear into her mouth.

"Mike A. He knows I'm a virgin. That's why he wouldn't go all the way with me. That's why

he hasn't said a word to me since Spring Break."
Cecily blows on her neon green fingertips. "My
virginity just, like, *radiates* from me. No amount
of perfume can cover up Essence of Virgin. Boys
know if you've done it before. They just know."
She blows on her fingers with more force.

"Essence of Virgin? Cecily, Jesus Christ."
Liz sighs.

"No, Liz. Mary! She's the virgin!" Cecily
retorts, now fanning her arms like a windmill.
"Anyway, I found this guy's card." She nods
her head in the direction of her desk, motioning
Liz to retrieve the card. "This guy provides a
service for girls in my situation. He takes your
virginity for just a small fee of fifty dollars. He's
a professional. He makes it quick and painless.
In and out. Done deal."

"Wait," Liz says as she sits up from Cecily's
bedroom floor. "Girls pay this guy to have sex
with him?"

"Yeah," Cecily replies. "He's a professional. I hear he's very good—the best in all of Braxton County. Look at his card."

"Where did you find this card?"

"In the locker room at school," Cecily explains. "There was a huge stack of them in there." Liz reluctantly examines the card with an embossed red rose. She flips it over.

Mike B

Professional Deviriginizer
"Deflower in less than one hour
—Guaranteed!"

Discounts available upon special request

"Oh yeah, he seems legit. And only fifty? I guess that's a fair price." Liz flips the card over again. "This must have been expensive to make. I wonder if I'll ever have my own business cards."

"I know, right? I just have to do it." Cecily swings her hand into her bedside table. "Crap! I smudged my nails!"

"I read if you hold cold glass bottles your nails dry faster," Liz says as she chews some more gummy bears.

In the kitchen Cecily pulls two bottles of Stella Artois from the refrigerator. "I don't even know why my mom has these. She only drinks vodka," Cecily says idly.

Liz pulls a bowl of leftover ground beef and Hamburger Helper from the microwave and stirs the reheated meal with a spoon. "That guy she was seeing last fall drank beer. Edward or whatever? That's probably why she still has them. What ever happened to him anyway?"

"He went back to his wife." In an attempt to deflect Liz's attention from the bowl of chopped meat, Cecily shakes the cold beer bottles like maracas. "Shall we?"

"Cecily Scott, it's 4:00 P.M. on a Monday."
Liz blows on a spoonful of Hamburger Helper.

"Whatever. We're fifteen now. We're basically
adults." Cecily cracks open a Stella.

"You've only been fifteen for a month."
Liz takes another bite of leftovers, pauses, and
places the bowl on the kitchen counter. "Fine. If
you're doing it, so will I. God, Cec."

The two best friends of six years clink their
bottles together and take a sip. "*Ew*," they say in
unison. They pour the remaining beer down the
sink and toss the bottles into the recycling bin
overflowing with empty vodka bottles.

"I've gotta get home for dinner, Cecily. Is
your mom working late again?" Liz asks as she
washes her bowl in the sink.

"Yeah, I think she finally closed the deal
on the Cedar Street house. It's about time. It's
been on the market for months. She should be
home soon. I'll call you later." Cecily opens the

refrigerator and closes it abruptly. "Hey, Liz," Cecily proposes, "maybe this professional sex guy does discounts for two girls at a time. You interested?"

"No thanks, Cecily. This is all you. Think of Mike A," Liz says as she cheerfully exits.

On the couch Cecily fiercely scrubs her nails with nail polish remover, turning her fingers a sickly shade of yellow as she retreats to the fond memory of being alone with her beloved Mike A in the backseat of the Ford Focus. Spring Break seems so long ago now. She knows what she has to do to win the affection of her charming prince. She must be deflowered.

"I'd like to solve the puzzle, Pat," a *Wheel of Fortune* contestant states. I'VE GOT A GOOD FEELING ABOUT THIS! The correct puzzle letters illuminate the television screen.

×

It's about ninety degrees as Cecily clicks

through the channels from the couch, sipping a plastic cup of vodka and cranberry juice. She's wearing stretch-denim shorts and a peach tank top embroidered with pale blue flowers. Her flip-flops have fallen from her feet and lay beside the couch.

"For just $19.99 a month, you will have the clear skin you were born to have!" the TV suggests.

The ceiling fan overhead blows stale air around the living room. Cecily adds ice cubes to her cocktail as the doorbell rings. Cecily perks up and goosebumps cover her entire body. A vision of Mike A's perfect smile appears in her head. She opens the front door.

A boy she does not recognize stands on her doorstep. He is wearing a backwards cap, tan cargo shorts, and a striped polo shirt with the emblem of an eagle on the right breast pocket. He is carrying a stately leather briefcase with gold clasps. Cecily towers over him, as he is about a foot shorter than she. "You must be Cecily," the boy says.

"And you must be Mike B," Cecily says as Mike B enters her home. They walk into the living room.

"Now we're cookin'!" a television chef shouts as he throws more chopped garlic into a sizzling skillet. Cecily sips from her plastic cup of vodka and cranberry juice.

"I'm on a tight schedule. Should we make our way to a bedroom?" Mike B says, clutching his briefcase.

"Sure, yeah." Cecily fumbles and nearly spills her drink. "Do you want anything? Water? Beer? Hamburger Helper?"

"No, thank you, Cecily. I am all set," Mike B responds.

Mike B rests his briefcase on Cecily's twin bed. Hours prior to this encounter, Cecily had made her bed for the first time in about three years. She hid her stuffed bear, Cocoa, in her closet. Mike B opens the briefcase to reveal a stopwatch, around fifty condoms, spermicidal lubricant, a small hand towel, a larger towel, a blindfold, a pack of Marlboro Reds, a candle, and some devices Cecily doesn't recognize.

"Are you going to use that, or am I?" Cecily points to the blindfold.

Mike B laughs. "That's up to you, Cecily. It's a courtesy I offer to my clients. Some girls ask to be blindfolded and others would prefer it if I am blindfolded. I get the job done either way. Or no one has to wear it at all."

"That's very generous of you." Cecily pauses and sips her vodka cranberry. "I guess we can leave the blindfold out of this whole ordeal. I'd like for both parties to be present."

"Great," says Mike B, placing the blindfold back into his briefcase. "You're not too harsh on the eyes anyway." Cecily ignores his professionally vacant compliment.

"Are you going to light that?" Cecily asks, pointing to the candle.

"I was planning on it. Its strong aroma tends to set the mood and allows clients to relax a little bit. It's vanilla scented. Did you know vanilla is an aphrodisiac? Do you know what an aphrodisiac is, Cecily?"

"Yes, I know what an aphrodisiac is, Mike B," Cecily asserts sardonically.

"And a healthy dose of cayenne pepper!" the televised chef shouts from the living room. *"Things are about to heat up!"*

"I'm a virgin, not a moron. Anyway, my mom doesn't like burning candles in the house. Her apartment burned down when she was younger. I'm relaxed enough. I don't need the candle. Let's get this over with, Mike B." She chugs the remaining alcohol and haphazardly tosses her cup onto her bedside table. "Should I pay you before or after our session?"

"Now is fine," Mike B says. "How much have you drunk today?"

"Enough to pay money to have sex with a short stranger carrying a briefcase from the Victorian era, apparently." She hands him a fifty dollar bill that she'd received from her aunt for her birthday last month.

Mike B lays the larger towel on Cecily's twin sized bed. "If all goes well, this will be sufficiently soiled with blood from your ruptured hymen. Don't be alarmed, it's perfectly natural." Cecily stops listening when she hears the word "sufficiently."

"Sorry," she apologizes, "I guess I'm nervous."

"Don't be nervous. This is a rite of passage and I'm not going to let anything bad happen to you. Trust me, Cecily." Mike B places his stopwatch on the table next to Cecily's empty cup. Now sufficiently inebriated, Cecily slouches on her twin bed covered by the same floral comforter she's had since she was six. Mike B sits down next to her and the bed squeaks. "I'm going to begin the foreplay now."

Cecily nods and glances at her empty cup on the end table, and then glances at her closet before meeting the gaze of Mike B's dark brown eyes. Her eyelashes flutter before she slowly gives herself to Mike B's soft, moist lips. Cecily opens her mouth wider as Mike B avidly juts his tongue deeper in. Cecily slides her hand beneath the short sleeve of her new lover's polo shirt. Mike B pulls away from Cecily's puckered lips. "I'm going to take your shirt off now. Lift up."

Cecily eagerly raises both arms above her head and Mike B removes her peach tank top and her white bra in one swift gesture. Feeling exposed and hot, Cecily removes Mike B's shirt too, revealing a tattoo of a family crest on his smooth chest. Mike B pulls Cecily into his bare chest, now dripping with sweat. Cecily's heart rate increases.

Mike B carefully lays Cecily onto her back as she shakily pants. "Are you wet?" Mike B asks as he pulls both her shorts and panties down to her ankles. His nimble fingers find Cecily's virgin loins and she sighs loudly. "You're doing great, Cecily. I'm going to lube your pussy up now." Mike B tenderly caresses Cecily and her eyes roll back with a new sense of uncertain pleasure. Vigorously rubbing Cecily, Mike B rips open a condom package with his teeth. He feverishly unravels a condom over his pulsating shaft and climbs on top of his client. Cecily studies the size of his member and feels grateful that it might not hurt so much. Kissing her softly, he coos, "Cecily, I'm going to enter you now. Are you ready?" He sucks on her left breast, which is slightly larger than her right breast. Overcome with desire, Cecily completely forgets how much she hates the asymmetry of her breasts.

Drenched in each other's sweat, they slip and gyrate with zeal. "Yes, I'm ready," Cecily hoarsely breathes.

"Say yes again," Mike B says in a firm, professional tone.

"Yes!" Cecily cries.

Mike B presses Cecily's body down and inserts himself into Virgin Cecily. She squeals, "Is it in?!" and clutches the pillow beneath her head.

"Almost," Mike B affirms. The pillow that was beneath Cecily's head is now covering her face and she holds it there trying to muffle her screeches. She takes long, shaky breaths. Mike B's member juts inside of her as throbbing pressure builds inside of Cecily.

Pinned to the wall beside her bed is a serene photograph of a girl's legs. Cecily has always found solace in the familiar white tennis shoes resting on top of overgrown blades of dewy morning grass. She jolts away from the photo and smothers her face with the pillow. Clenching the pillow with all her might, Princess Cecily is transported to her palace. Mike A bows while Princess Cecily elegantly curtseys and the distinguished string quartet begins to play the first waltz. Mike A gracefully twirls Princess Cecily around the ballroom as her powder blue ball gown cascades around her willowy frame. As their beloved monarchs glide effortlessly across the ballroom, royal subjects clap and cheer, for everyone in Princess Cecily's kingdom is filled with joy. Fireworks crackle over the castle and winged ponies dance in the air.

Suddenly a wet warmth erupts and Cecily Scott takes the pillow off of her face. To her dismay, she does not see Mike A's perfect body but the distorted face of her short business partner. He is wearing a grimace she has never seen before. He begins to thrust with more enthusiasm. "I'm in, Cecily," he whimpers. "You're doing so well."

Cecily hazily stares at Mike B's face of undeniable passion. Turned on and confused, she moves her hips with his. The sound of their bodies slamming against each other masks the squeaking of the twin bed.

"Cecily, I'm going to cum soon," Mike B breathes as he grabs Cecily's left breast again. Cecily shakes. Mike B pumps faster and faster and Cecily closes her eyes again, until suddenly he releases a skillful growl. Cecily tries not to laugh at the tremendous sound erupting from her devirginizer. His pumping slows down and Mike B finally collapses on top of Cecily. Together, they steady their breathing. Cecily stares at the ceiling.

"So that's it?" Cecily asks quietly, covered in sweat, hymen blood, and spermicidal lubricant. She wishes she had lit that vanilla scented candle. She also wishes her mom would install an AC unit in the house.

"Yeah." Mike B rolls over, grabbing his polo shirt from the floor. "Congratulations, you're officially deflowered." He looks at the stopwatch on the end table. "And in just eleven minutes! Do I have yet another satisfied customer?"

Mike B is almost completely dressed. "Oh, and I'll take this off your hands. Cleanup is included in my service." He lifts Cecily's legs and retrieves the sufficiently soiled towel from beneath her.

Astonished by the deep shade of maroon the once-white towel is, Cecily coughs, "Yes, I'm a satisfied customer."

"Great, Cecily. You were great. Superb. Welcome to womanhood. You're now free of your Virgin Essence. Can't you feel it?" Mike B reaches into his wallet. "Here, distribute these to your friends. I offer discounted services to referring customers."

"You offer other services?" Cecily asks.

"Oh yeah, Cecily. My clients pay large sums for anal penetration. Would you be interested in that today? Fifty percent off for you, just because you were such a trooper. So lovely."

Cecily's groin throbs with pain. "Maybe some other time," Cecily grumbles as she takes the card from Mike B's clammy hands.

"Very well. I have a few more appointments this evening anyway." He snaps his briefcase closed. "You're probably going to feel sore for a few days. Take these." Mike B hands Cecily two white pills.

"No, thanks. I'll be fine."

"Suit yourself, Cecily. I can see myself out. It has been a pleasure doing business with you."

"Likewise," Cecily responds, and Mike B, the Professional Devirginizer, is already out the front door.

Cecily lifts her sore body from her twin bed. Feeling incredibly sore yet vaguely regal, she dresses herself with an oversized tee and walks to her closet. She takes Cocoa Bear out and hugs him tightly, and then lovingly places him on her devirginized bed. She looks at her devirginized bedroom, her empty cup of vodka, her childhood toy on her twin bed. She picks Cocoa Bear up and places him back in the closet. Cecily gazes into her mirror as she attempts to finger-comb her bleached, now matted hair. She glances at the closet once more and imagines her future with Mike A.

From the living room the television chef boasts, *"And that's how it's done! Another mind-blowing home-cooked meal made in just under sixty minutes!"* The studio audience goes wild.

Mike C

The hallways of West Braxton High are crowded and hot. The final bell has just rung and the student body is now in weekend mode; running amuck, yelling, screaming. Even the teachers are eager to leave the building. Cecily jiggles the lock on her locker. It takes her about eighty-two tries before she can ever unlock it. As she struggles, her body tenses and goosebumps prickle her arms because a foreign hand is squeezing her shoulder. She whips around, aghast. An earthly Adonis is glowing brilliantly before her. Her physics book falls to the floor.

"Hello, Cecily Scott." Mike A beams.

"Hi, yourself. Can I help you with something?"

"What's that supposed to mean?" Mike A's beautiful body hunches over as he retrieves the book from the floor.

"I don't know. I haven't spoken to you since Spring Break." Cecily snatches her book from Mike A. "I feel like you've been avoiding me."

"What are you talking about? I've been prepping for the SAT. If I don't get a scholarship, I can't go to college, and I've been trying to maintain my GPA." He touches her shoulder again. "I've been really busy, Cecily Scott."

Cecily Scott tilts her head, feeling a vague sense of redemption.

"You seem different. Did you do something with your hair?" Mike A asks.

I knew it, Cecily thinks to herself and silently thanks her Professional Devirginzer. "Not recently, but I've been doing Pilates," she effortlessly lies.

"Wow, it shows. You're kind of glowing." Mike A adjusts the cap on his perfect head. "Some of the Boys are having a little shindig at Mike C's poolhouse tonight. I was wondering if you'd be interested—"

"Definitely," Cecily blurts out.

"Cool. You don't need to bring anything but a bathing suit. I'll probably swing by around six. Here's the address and the directions to the poolhouse. I drew the map myself. I hope it's not too confusing." Mike A hands Cecily a folded piece of looseleaf.

"Oh, Cedar Street. My mom just sold a house on that street! Liz is going to flip!"

"Yeah, pretty ritzy neighborhood. Oh, and another thing," Mike A adds. "It's kind of exclusive. I only have a Plus One."

"But Liz is my best friend…" Cecily pauses as Mike A stares deep into her soul with his mesmerizing eyes of azure. "Okay, I'll see you at six."

"Count on it, Cecily Scott," Mike A says before vanishing into the chaotic hallway of West Braxton High. Cecily floats all the way home.

"Hi, Sweetie. No mail today, but Liz called just five minutes ago!" Cecily's mother shouts from the kitchen. A strong aroma of burning food fills their home. "I'm making chicken and rice for dinner. It's so nice to be home before nightfall for once. I thought we could have a nice meal, just the two of us." Cecily's mother adds more vodka to her vodka soda. Cecily descends from Cloud Nine and begins to wilt with contrition.

"Mom, I love you. More than anything you know that," Cecily explains, wary of her fragile mother, "but Mike A invited me to a very small, very tame pool party and it starts at six on the dot and I know it sounds extreme but I think he's The One."

Cecily's mother releases an exuberant, harrowing laugh and nearly knocks over a pot of simmering rice. "*The One?* Cecily, you just turned fifteen." She sips her cocktail. "No one finds The One at fifteen years old. It takes years of trial and error to find..." Cecily's mother places her drink on the counter and uses her unpolished fingers to make disdainful air quotes, "...The One." She cackles again as boiling rice overflows onto the stovetop.

Refraining from confessing to her bitter mother that she does not want to end up broken, alone, hopeless, and exhausted like her, Cecily sighs as she turns down the gas on the stove. She hands her mother the glass of vodka and assents with a sweet smile. "I'll never find out if

I don't try."

"What's the point?" Cecily's mother takes a swig of her cocktail.

"Mom, please. I will be home at ten and I swear on my life that we will do Mom and Cecily bonding dinner tomorrow," Cecily bargains. "It's Saturday! You don't have to work, right?"

"I have to show a few houses tomorrow, but, okay, sweetheart. We can reschedule if this Mike A means so much to you. And what did I tell you about swearing on my only daughter's life, Cecily Nicole?"

"I'll love you forever, Ricardo!" a soap opera actress cries from the living room. *"I'll never let you go!"*

"You're the best, Mom! Thank you!" Cecily leaps across the kitchen to hug her mother with enthusiasm. "And it's on Cedar Street!"

"Oh, how *luxurious*," Cecily's mother drawls, failing to conceal her contempt. "Will

Liz be there too? Is that why she called?"

"Of course," Cecily lies. "We do everything together. You know that."

"Of course. Okay, go get ready, but please eat something first."

"I had an enormous lunch," Cecily lies again.

"Ricardo, how could you do this to me? You told me you loved me!" the television sobs. *"You told me you would love me until we were both dead."*

Wearing plastic flip-flops and a mint green sundress, a daisy print bikini underneath, Cecily watches her mother drive away and begins to trek up Mike C's unpaved narrow driveway. The long, winding path weaves through hundreds of pine trees that barricade the most stunning house she has ever seen. *Camelot,* she thinks to herself. Carrying Mike A's hand drawn map, she makes her way to the heavily wooded backyard. *I'm Mike A's Plus One,* she hums in her head. *I'm exclusively his.* However, Mike A's illegible map leads Cecily off the path and she is now tramping through the woods. Treading through endless brush, Cecily begins to panic, fearing that she will never find her way out of Mike C's dense backyard. She listens carefully and hears the faint sounds of music and splashing pool water. Gathering her composure, Cecily tosses Mike A's useless map and finds her way out of the wilderness. At last Cecily emerges from the woods and spots the pack of Brax Boys and their Plus Ones standing around the gated pool. The poolhouse is seven times larger than Cecily's home on the other side of town. Overweight and overweening, Mike C cannonballs from the diving board and everyone cheers.

Cecily creeps into the pool area and suddenly she is invisible to her peers and Mike A is nowhere to be found. She makes her way to a long table stocked with liquors worth more than her mother's mortgage and fixes herself a vodka cranberry. Yet to be acknowledged by anyone at the party, Cecily leans against the pewter gate and takes a few long, deep sips of her beverage. She then finishes another and the Brax pack is chanting, *"Hot Tub! Hot Tub! Hot Tub!"* Cecily is about to pour her third concoction when she sees that Mike A has just stepped out of the poolhouse.

"Did someone get lucky?" Mike C shouts as he attempts to pull his massive body onto a pool float.

"Dude, no. I was cleaning up a broken flower vase in the dining room." Mike A places a bouquet of lilies into an ice bucket. "You're welcome." Mike A motions a limp salute to Mike C, who is still struggling with the pool float, and strolls over to Cecily's vodka cranberry station.

"For you, m'lady." Mike A presents Cecily with a flower from the ice bucket.

"Wow, thank you." Cecily blushes. "I love

lilies." Her cheeks are hot and cranberry red.

"So you made it," Mike A congratulates Cecily as she glides the sweet gift over her nose and lips.

"Yeah, I made it. Here I am at the poolhouse. Your map was very precise." Cecily reaches for a bottle of Jack Daniels. "You're a natural cartographer."

"Are you insulting my handwriting, Cecily Scott?"

"No, I'm insulting your sense of direction," Cecily jokes, "but I can't blame you for that. You're a guy." She cracks the bottle of Jack open with ease. "Thank you for inviting me," she says in earnest, "and for making me your Plus One."

"My pleasure, Cecily Scott."

"I've never had whiskey before," Cecily announces before taking a swig straight from the bottle.

"Chicken Fight!!!" Mike C yells from the pool as two girls straddle the shoulders of two robust Brax Boys. Mike C pops a bottle of champagne and showers the two mounted girls. The party roars as the girls in fluorescent string bikinis slap each other repeatedly. Two more Brax Boys sneak behind the fighting girls and untie their respective saddled girls' tops. *"CHICK-EN FIGHT. CHICK-EN FIGHT. CHICK-EN FIGHT."* The topless girls progress from slapping to punching. "Play nice, little chickies," Mike C warns, puffing a cigar. "You still have two more rounds."

Cecily shields her eyes from the match. "Are those girls having fun?" she asks Mike A.

"It sure looks like it!" Still mounted on Brax Boys, the topless girls are now kissing wildly and sloppily. *"MAKE OUT! MAKE OUT! MAKE OUT!"*

"Want to see the pad?" Mike A suggests as he fixes himself a whiskey ginger ale. "There's a TV the size of an SUV inside,"

Mike A says, directing Cecily's attention to the gargantuan poolhouse.

"Sure," Cecily says as she tries a sip of tequila. "I love TVs."

"Let's get ready to rumble!!!!" the massive TV bellows as Mike A and Cecily enter the poolhouse where a few of their peers are funneling beer.

"You're right," Cecily concurs. "That's an enormous TV."

"Told you!" Mike A grins and gently squeezes Cecily's shoulder. Cecily melts.

"New girls have to funnel," a Brax Boy says to Cecily.

"She's good," Mike A insists.

Cecily grabs the funnel from the Brax Boy's hand. "Why not?" She wraps her freshman mouth around the wet plastic tube as the cold beer rushes down her throat. The crowd goes wild.

A Brax Boy hands Cecily a shot glass.

"And some bourbon to wash it down." Cecily swiftly shoots it back and curtsies before she and Mike A exit the TV room and climb the spiral staircase.

"Impressive, Cecily Scott. What other hidden talents do you have?" He nudges Cecily in the arm.

"I wouldn't call funneling a little beer a talent," Cecily slurs, nudging Mike A noticeably harder than his initial flirtatious nudge. "Why didn't you funnel too? It was exhilarating! I feel great!"

"I'm pacing myself." Mike A firmly wraps his arm around Cecily's waist and guides her up the stairs.

In what appears to be the game room, four girls in bikinis lay flat across a billiard table so Brax Boys can cover their bodies with whipped cream before licking it off.

"New girl's next!" a Brax Boy shouts,

shaking a can of Redi-Whip.

"That's not necessary," Mike A asserts, pulling Cecily closer to his strong, perfect body. Cecily is grateful and somewhat dizzy. She is his Plus One.

"You her dad or something? At least let her have a jello shot," the Brax Boy condescends. "New Girl, want to ask your daddy if he'll let you have some jello?"

"I don't have a father and my name is Cecily Nicole Scott," she snaps before grabbing two cups of jello. "Thanks." Cecily shoots one and hands the other to Mike A.

Impressed with the New Girl, the Brax Boy raises his Redi-Whip can and smiles. "You're a champ, Cecily Nicole Scott. Enjoy the party."

Mike A and his Plus One enter the keg room. *"KEG STAND! KEG STAND! KEG STAND!"* A gaggle of Brax Boys hold a girl upside down over the keg and pump beer into her mouth.

"New Girl—"

"Yes, I'm the new girl," Cecily interrupts and turns to Mike A. "Hold me up?" Cecily holds onto the edges of the cold keg and chugs as Mike A begrudgingly holds her legs in the air, making sure her mint dress doesn't fall over her head. He then carefully places her feet into her plastic flip-flops.

"Okay, she's had enough," Mike A announces.

"Dad knows best!" Cecily hiccups, clutching the arm of her chivalrous date. With a beer in each hand, Cecily and Mike A exit the keg room.

"You're really hitting it off with the Boys," Mike A states.

"I guess so," Cecily slurs. "Sorry about the 'Dad knows best' comment. It just kind of came out." She looks into Mike A's blue eyes. "It wasn't nice or funny." She apologetically traces Mike A's arm with her index finger.

"I forgive you." Mike A holds Cecily's hand in his. "Do you want to go somewhere quiet?" Mike A whispers.

"I hear there's a hot tub. Is that true?" Cecily beams. "I'm already wearing a bathing suit, you know." She leans into Mike A's gleaming eyes and bats her lashes.

"It's true." Mike A sweeps Cecily off her feet and carries her down the hall.

Mike A opens the door to a steamy room with floor to ceiling windows surrounding a luxurious hot tub. The jets have already been turned on. Mike A tenderly lowers Cecily to her feet and she shuts the door behind them. She walks to the window overlooking the woods. "This is unreal. Liz would just die," she gasps, feeling guilty for excluding her best friend. She pictures her unknowing best friend getting an early start on her homework with a pint of ice cream on her desk. *This party doesn't seem very "exclusive" either...* Liz will understand, Cecily concludes, when she too has found The One. And besides, Liz probably wouldn't have much fun anyway. She's a virgin and doesn't even drink. Cecily removes her dress. She places her lily on the marble tabletop and eases into the hot water.

Mike A slides into the simmering tub beside Cecily. "Is it wrong that I wanted to be alone with you?" He grazes Cecily's thigh with his own and runs his fingers along her jawline to her chin. They lock yearning eyes. Cecily's guilt disintegrates into the bubbling water as it morphs into pure desire.

"You did?" Cecily squeaks. "I mean, it isn't wrong."

With fluid control Mike A leans toward Cecily's ready body and slowly kisses her jello-stained mouth. Massaging Mike A's tongue with her own, blood rushes to her loins and she gives in to him. Floating on top of Mike A, Cecily presses her body against his, wrapping her limbs around his torso like a koala to a tree branch. She kisses him deeper as she pulsates below. Mike A squeezes Cecily tighter and playfully bites her lip. Embraced in climbing passion, the wet lovers' unified breathing escalates to feverish panting.

Tracing Cecily's daisy print bikini top, Mike A inches to the nape her of her neck and with a swift maneuver her top is now floating on the surface of the foggy water. Cecily tilts her head back as Mike A gently nibbles her supple, albeit lopsided breasts. She quivers and tugs at Mike A's swim trunks as he squeezes feverishly.

Cecily guides Mike A's experienced hands to her daisy print briefs. She sighs as the other half of her swimsuit disappears into the water. Mike A removes his swim trunks and pushes his hard member against the inner crease of

Cecily's thigh. Their naked bodies glide with fiery vigor. Dizzy with pleasure and jello shots, Cecily's body suddenly tenses and she grabs onto the sides of the hot tub.

"Is everything okay?" Mike A breathes into Cecily's neck.

"Yeah, this is fantastic. I feel like I'm dreaming. You feel so good." Cecily jolts. "I'm not dreaming, right?"

"Cecily Scott, if you were dreaming, would you be able to feel this?" With his nimble fingers, Mike A tenderly circles Cecily's most sensitive spot, which she never knew existed until this very moment.

"I'm not dreaming," Cecily moans. "I want you inside of me."

Mike A grins and reaches into a basket of condoms beside the tub. He wraps his beautiful shaft with an extra large condom. His moist hands cup Cecily's cranberry blushed face as he kisses her deeply and passionately. He caresses Cecily with his firm penis where his fingers have been massaging her before. Cecily jerks as the teasing becomes unbearable. Throbbing with titillation, she reaches under water and pushes Mike A inside. He moans with intense pleasure and pulls her closer. Cecily recoils as Mike A slowly thrusts, deeper with each pump. "Oh my god," Cecily slurs. He pumps harder. "Don't stop. I want more!" Cecily cries, digging her nails into his shoulder blades. Mike A joyfully plunges deeper and lets out a shaky moan. Cecily spreads her legs as far as she can to take all of her passionate lover. He grips Cecily's torso and pants into Cecily's neck as he pounds with effort. A tense hotness overcomes both lovers as water spills from the tub onto the floor. Cecily rises to Mike A's thrill and then spasms with zealous delight. "Oh my god!" She guzzles as water splashes into her mouth. Embracing his fair lover, Mike A penetrates harder and faster until an eruption of bliss fills the steamy room. Trembling, Mike A gives a forceful thrust and yells, "Yes, yes, YES." Still entwined, their bodies relax and their breathing slows down. Mike A kisses Cecily gently on the lips as he pulls out.

"Another hidden talent, Cecily Scott," Mike A says, catching his breath. "You were amazing." He kisses her glistening cheek.

"Likewise," Cecily nods, heart still racing. "This is better than a dream." She closes her eyes and wilts into Mike A, cradling her like a baptized baby.

"Is it hot in here?" Cecily asks, sweating profusely.

"Well, we are in a hot tub."

"I think I'm going to be sick." Cecily jumps out of the tub and projects red liquid onto the floor.

"Oh, no. I shouldn't have done this." Mike A fumbles out of the hot tub. "I'm so sorry for taking advantage of you, Cecily." Mike A covers Cecily's wet, naked body with a towel and holds her hair back. She heaves.

"You didn't take advantage of me," Cecily crumbles. "I wanted this...I've wanted this for so long...better than a dream." She pukes again. "This is the best night of my life. I feel... enchanted." Another spew.

"Yes, this is certainly enchanting."

Cecily attempts to stand. "I'm not sick anymore," she says bluntly. "Should we go back to the party?"

Mike A wipes Cecily's face with a towel and then kisses her on the forehead. "We're getting you a ride home, Cecily Scott," he declares while dressing her with care.

"But I'm fine!" Cecily pleads as her body slinks to the floor.

Mike A empties an ice bucket into the hot tub and places it in front of Cecily "We have

Jared on call tonight. He'll be happy to leave anyway. You need to drink lots of water and sleep this off. I should probably head home too. I have a landscaping job in the morning." He rubs her back. "Partying isn't easy, Cecily Scott. Next time, try to pace yourself...and try to aim for the bucket."

Through tears Cecily squints into the dramatic blue eyes of Mike A before throwing up into his lap.

Moments later Cecily awakes in the backseat of Jared's car. "Where's Mike A?" she asks the driver.

"He just went to say 'bye to the Boys," Jared responds, peering into the pool party. "Should be back any minute now." He opens his glove box and turns to Cecily. "Here, take this." He extends his arm to Cecily. "It's my card. If you ever run into trouble and need a safe ride home, do not hesitate to call." Cecily takes Jared's card.

Coachman With A Corolla
Designated Driver for Damsels,
Dames and Drunks
Call Toll Free:
1-800-GET-HOME

Cecily puts the card in her wallet and opens the car door to throw up again.

"Sorry that took so long," Mike A says as he joins Cecily in the backseat of Jared's car. "One of the Boys smashed a bottle over his head. Blood everywhere." He strokes Cecily's hair. "You might feel like shit tomorrow, but a hangover beats a trip to the ER." Cecily lets out an incomprehensible whimper and nuzzles into her gallant darling, still clutching her tattered lily.

"You still look pretty." Mike A pets Cecily's feeble arm. "Even covered in jello puke." Though nauseous and frazzled, Cecily's heart leaps with joy. *He's The One,* she thinks before fading into darkness.

"Cecily, wake up. We're here."

Cecily opens her drowsy eyes and looks out the window. They are parked in her mother's driveway.

"Look at that—home before you can turn into a pumpkin," Mike A jokes as he helps Cecily out of the car.

"Thank you for everything. I'm sorry I threw up on you and the floor and that whole basket of condoms and anything else. I had an amazing time."

"It's been truly enchanting, Cecily Scott." He kisses her chastely on her front porch and then hops into the front seat of Jared's car.

"Thanks for the ride!" Cecily waves to Jared with her flower from Mike A.

The car drives away and Cecily vomits onto the lawn. *This is not a dream,* she thinks. *I'm in love.*

Mike D

"He didn't answer." Cecily slams the phone down as bleach soaks through her foiled hair.

"Oh, wow. I thought the fourteenth time would be the charm," Liz says sarcastically, shaking Parmesan cheese onto a thick slice of pizza.

"What is As I Lay Dying?*"* a contestant asks.

"That is correct," Alex Trebek answers. *"As I Lay Dying, by William Faulkner."*

"I'll take Southern Gothic for 400, Alex."

"You need to stop calling, Cecily. He's going to get your number blocked if he hasn't already." Liz takes a bite of pizza. "He's probably busy. He cares about grades, right? Finals Week is approaching, you know."

"It's been two weeks since the pool party and Mike A has not said a word to me. Everytime he sees me he walks in the other direction. I don't care if it's Finals Week. We had sex! He said I was amazing…" Cecily fights back a tear. "I thought he was The One."

"I mean, you puked all over him. Maybe—"

"Liz, I told you not to bring that up." Cecily stomps her foot. "Oh my god, I am never drinking alcohol again. Never, ever again. I swear on your life."

"Please do not swear on my life, Cec," Liz snaps with a mouthful of soggy dough.

"Sorry. I swear on my own life to never

drink alcohol again."

"That's a bold statement."

"I don't care if the entire student body thinks I'm lame," Cecily exclaims. "I would do anything for love!"

Liz idly flips through the channels. "I don't know. Maybe he's gay.

Cecily ponders this notion. "You think?"

"No."

"I'm never drinking again."

"Good idea." Liz goes on chewing. "And I can't believe you didn't invite me either. I would have invited you in a heartbeat. And what if Mike A hadn't gotten you a ride home? What would you have done?" Liz lectures.

"You're right. I'm an idiot." Cecily sits next to Liz on the living room couch and leans her head on her shoulder. "I'm sorry I didn't invite you."

"It's okay, Cec." Liz wraps her arm around her defeated best friend. "You're lucky I love you." She pops the last piece of crust into her mouth. "And frozen pizza. My mom put everyone in our house on a strict no carbohydrate diet. It's unbearable."

"Well, carbs make you fat," Cecily says to her best friend of eight years. "Not that you're fat or anything." Cec reaches for the phone. "Just one more try."

"Hey, it's your funeral." Liz raises the television volume.

"I'll take Royals for 800." The Daily Double sound plays as an incessant busy signal blares from the phone receiver into Cecily's ear.

×

The final bell rings and Cecily struggles to open her locker, as she does several times a day, five days a week.

"You have to be gentle," a low voice says

from behind her.

"Excuse me?" Cecily snaps with frustration. She looks over her shoulder. A tall, blonde boy is towering over her. He is the most popular boy in the entire school. Mike D, a senior, is the captain of the lacrosse team as well as the chess club. He is the founder of the school's Young Democrat Society and the chief editor of the school newspaper. A small wing of West Braxton High is dedicated to his philanthropist father.

"You have to be gentle with these old locks or they'll never budge," handsome Mike D says. "What's your combo?"

"I'm not telling you my locker combination," Liz blurts, still frustrated and hot.

"I'm going to Columbia in a month. I'm not interested in your algebra book," Mike D says.

"I take advanced placement calculus, actually," Cecily retorts. "It's 37-42-5."

Mike D gently spins the lock and the metal

door opens with ease. "See?" Mike D smiles. "You can't force anything, or you'll never get what you want. You have to be gentle. You have to convince people, or in this case, locks, that it's their idea. This lock wants to open, you just need to give it some time to decide that's what it wants to do."

"Thanks," Cecily says as she puts her books away. She extends her arm to Mike D. "I'm Cecily. We haven't met, I don't think."

"Cecily, we met at C's party, but I think you were a few beer funnels in by that time." He shakes her hand. His hands are soft and his grip is firm. "I'm Mike D."

"Right, that party." Cecily tries her best to disappear. "Well, thanks for the locker help and subtle life advice." She closes her locker.

Mike D lingers. "Yeah, C's parties get a little crazy sometimes, but it's all in good fun. You've just gotta pace yourself."

"So I'm told," Cecily says, still trying to disappear. "I'm never drinking again."

"Been there. Alcohol is poison. That's why I stick with grass." Mike D fiddles with his elegant hands. "Hey, are you busy right now? Do you want to hang out? No booze at all. We can just drive around, take in the scenery, what have you. The weather is perfect today, don't you think? I mean, no pressure."

"I don't know. I have to study for finals." Cecily pauses and remembers that the most popular person in all of Braxton County is asking her to hang out. Every girl in town dreams of this, and Mike A would be sick with jealousy if he found out. He'd beg Cecily to be with him. "Well, I guess I could, but I need to call my mom first."

"Of course. Call your mom and meet me in the lot. I'll park out front."

"I'll be right out." The crowded hallway

parts like the Red Sea as messianic Mike D walks out the lobby doors.

Cecily stands at a phone booth next to the cafeteria. "What happened with Mike A? Did you guys break up?" Cecily's mother's asks.

"Sort of."

"Mike D? His father is the head ER doctor at St. Jude's, right?"

"Correct."

"Okay, perfect, because I probably won't be home until late tonight. I've been trying to get this listing for weeks. No one wants to give listings to real estate agents, just brokers, or they want to sell on their own. This market is madness."

"Mom, I don't have any more quarters for the phone…"

"All right, sweet pea. See you at home. Don't take any wooden nickels." Cecily's mother pulls from a bank of around ten clichés she likes to say. Comforted by her mother's meaningless line, Cecily rolls her eyes.

"See you at ten. Love you, Mom."

"I love you to the moon and back, Cecily Nicole." Another one of her sayings Cecily cannot bring herself to resent.

Cecily scrambles to the front of the parking lot to see Mike D standing outside of his blue Mustang convertible. "Allow me," says Mike D as he opens the passenger door for Cecily.

"I've never been in a convertible before," Cecily admits.

"Oh, it's the best. I'm trying to get the most out of it before I move to New York. I have to leave this baby behind when I move. I'm a safe driver, don't worry."

"I'm not worried." Cecily buckles her seatbelt as Mike D gracefully shifts gears, exiting campus.

"So, do you have summer plans?" Mike D asks.

"Not really. My mom wants me to get a job, but I have no experience. I can't get a job without experience and I can't get experience if no one will hire me. I can babysit, I guess, though kids don't really like me."

"I find that hard to believe," Mike D says with a laugh.

"No, they really don't! I smiled at a baby just the other day and it instantly started to cry!"

"I bet that baby would be somewhat offended to know that you referred to him or her as an 'it.'" Mike D smiles.

Cecily pulls her windblown hair to one side and smiles back. "Do you have summer plans?"

"Just this! I'm moving to the City in a month. I'm trying to take in country life. Nature is sparse in the Big Apple." He accelerates and shifts gears again.

"I've only been to New York City once, when I was eight. My aunt took me and my cousins to see *The Nutcracker* a week before Christmas."

"Oh yeah? How was that?"

"It was perfect and I didn't want it to end. I sat at the edge of my seat the entire time. I fell in love with ballet. I begged my mom to let me take lessons after that, but she told me I'd regret it."

"Why'd she think that?"

"She used to be an actress. Or she tried to be an actress anyway. That's how she met my dad, I guess. In Hollywood. He was a director. Or maybe he still is. I don't know. Anyway, she told me show business is no place for women. My dancing career would be over by the time I turned twenty-two. I was eight at the time, so I resented her, but she's probably right."

"Your mom must be a looker," Mike D says as he checks the sideview mirror.

"She drinks a lot."

"Life is a long, winding road. It doesn't get much easier as you get older. My parents are addicted to prescription pills. Tons of them, just so they can function." He stops at a four-way stop. "She must be proud of you, though, for taking AP Calc and everything."

"I don't think she knows any of the classes I take. She's never asked." Cecily sticks her hand out the car and lets the warm air beat through her fingers. "I remember the smell of New York City the most. It was cold, metallic, kind of, but there was a crisp, burning smell too. Hot dogs, maybe. Or pretzels. That's all I remember of the City though. I mean besides the Rat King and the sugar plum fairies."

Mike D turns left onto a road Cecily does not recognize. "That's pretty accurate. There are plenty of fairies and rats in New York." Mike D reaches into the center console and pulls out a joint. "You feel like getting lost?"

"Sure, but not too lost," Cecily says.

The Mustang scuttles onto a road Cecily

has never noticed in the fifteen years she has lived in Braxton County. Sunlight speckles the road through the elm trees with which it is lined. Relaxed, Cecily breathes in the early summer air and lets the sun graze her face.

"Do you want some of this?" Mike D asks, passing her his tightly rolled joint.

Cecily shakes her head. "I'm okay, thanks."

"No worries." Mike D takes a drag. "So, what's the deal with you and Mike A? You seemed pretty close at the poolhouse."

Cecily jolts from her convertible bliss. "I don't really want to talk about that."

"Got it. We don't have to talk at all. Let's just take it all in. Let's cruise." Mike D turns the radio on.

"Your happily ever after is right around the corner. We will give you cash for gold! Call toll free now! CASH FOR GOLD!" a man yells from the speakers.

"Do you like the Dead?" Mike D asks,

inserting a CD into the car stereo.

"Yeah," Cecily lies. "They're okay." She has never heard the Grateful Dead before.

The car weaves through dusty dirt roads. Cecily notices a family of deer in the distance and puts her feet on the dashboard. She feels safe and serene as Jerry Garcia serenades the shady road.

"Sunshine, daydream, walking in the tall trees, going where the wind blows…" Jerry sings. The air suddenly gets cooler and the trees get thicker.

"Do you hear that?" Mike D asks, lowering the music.

"Hear what?"

"Listen." Mike D slows the car. "It's a waterfall. Maybe a mile from here." He pulls the car over. "You feel like exploring?"

"Why not?" Cecily grins.

They venture down a beaten footpath in the woods. Picking wildflowers along the way,

Mike D holds Cecily's hand as they cross over scattered ponds, holding branches for her as she stumbles along. As Mike D predicted, the waterfall appears in the distance about a mile into the woods.

The trees open to a majestic field of wooded greenery. The air smells of lilac; pink and purple perennials sprinkle the floor. A rainbow spouts from the booming waterfall. Cool mist tickles their faces and coats the forest with sparkling dew.

"Oh, wow," Cecily gasps.

"It's not so bad at all," Mike D agrees. They sit on a moist log perfectly placed next to a willow tree. Mike D skillfully braids his hand-picked wildflowers with his gentle hands. "Thanks for coming here with me. It's nice to get lost with someone else. I'm grateful to find such a beautiful place with a beautiful person." He places a flower crown on Cecily's head.

"Thanks," Cecily blushes. "I'm having

a really nice time. I never do stuff like this. I mean, I can't drive, so it's kind of difficult to get lost, but this is much better than watching *Jeopardy* in my living room."

"You can get lost anywhere if you just let yourself. You probably do it all the time, but you just don't realize it. You can't force it. Just let it happen. Let your mind take you places you've never been." Mike D shrugs. "*Jeopardy* is cool though. Better than all that reality TV bullshit."

"I guess."

Mike D wraps his arm around Cecily and she falls into his chest, listening to his slow, steady heartbeat. "Maybe we'll see some sugar plum fairies if we look hard enough," he quips.

"This feels good. I like getting lost." Cecily breathes in the smell of Mike D's subtle cologne enhanced by the waterfall mist. "This is embarrassing and forward, but I want to kiss you," Cecily whispers.

"I want to kiss you too," Mike D says.

A sincere smile dances across Cecily's face and she leans into Mike D's dazzling kiss. *Mike A who?* she thinks to herself as she melts into pleasure.

Holding each other close, their passion rises. Cecily removes the linen shirt from the most popular boy in Braxton County. Mike D then spreads the shirt onto a patch of soft clover. "I know it's not a California King but it's probably more comfortable than this wet log." He lays Cecily onto the makeshift bed of linen and clover. "Is this okay?"

"This is okay," Cecily says, pulling her own shirt over her head, pulling Mike D's firm, tan torso toward her exposed body. As fiery momentum builds, Cecily tears the rest of her clothing off and fumbles with the button on Mike D's pants. His hard-on is undeniable. He thrusts as sweet beads of sweat drip onto Cecily's chest. She digs her fingers into his lower back, pulling him closer, and he pecks her neck with slow, hot kisses.

"Do you have a condom?" Cecily coos.

"I do, but do you want to do this?" Mike D asks politely.

"I do," she whimpers.

Mike D reaches into his leather wallet and rips open a condom wrapper. Eager with desire, Cecily effortlessly unzips his pants and pulls them off. He places them behind her head for a pillow.

"Can I do it?" Cecily asks, driven wild with passion. She takes the condom from his hand and slides it onto his hard shaft.

"You're incredible," Mike D says, gently sliding into Cecily. They moan in harmony as a hummingbird pollinates an orchid beside them. Falling into bliss, Cecily clenches a handful of clover in delight as Mike D pumps deeper. He then takes her by the throat and squeezes. *Is this normal?* she wonders, gasping for air. She squirms as Mike D's grip tightens around her neck.

"Fuck, you're so fucking hot," he grunts. Suddenly he pulls out and turns Cecily around to all fours. The pants that were once Cecily's pillow are now being tied around her wrists behind her back. She kisses the damp soil as Mike D enters her from behind, squeezing her breasts. Cecily yelps as his enormous penis hits her in an extremely sensitive place. Her eyes water as she arches her back as far as she can stand it. Mike D pulls her hair into a ponytail and tugs. Her flower crown topples from her head and vanishes into the woodland floor. "You fucking whore. Do you like that? I know you like that. You love my hard dick inside of your tight pussy."

Cecily's eyes widen as her head is pulled all the way back. Mike D spanks her three times. "You slut. You little fucking slut. Tell me you're a dirty slut."

"I'm a dirty slut."

He spanks her harder. "You're going to make me cum."

"Are you coming, Princess?" Mike A shouts. He is standing in a vast field of daffodils next to his faithful white steed. "We cannot disappoint our subjects. They're waiting for us."

From a tall stone tower, Princess Cecily cranes her neck out the window. "Yes, my love, but I've locked myself in this chamber again. The lock will not budge!"

"Again? Princess, we've been over this. You turn the key clockwise twice and counter clockwise once. You have to be gentle!"

"It won't unlock, my fair prince. I'm afraid I'll be in this tower forever!" Princess Cecily weeps.

"Do not cry, my princess. I will climb this mighty tower to save you. Compared to the fire-breathing dragon I slayed to win the King's approval, this is a warm summer breeze." Mike A, dressed in a suit of royal blue, climbs the royal tower with ease. Entering through the window, he holds his beloved princess in his strong arms. "I would climb to the moon and back for you, my love."

"My hero!" Princess Cecily exclaims. The royal couple embrace as bluebirds place a delicate tiara atop Cecily's sovereign head.

"Bitch, I'm going to cum on your tits," Mike D utters amidst heavy breathing. He flips Cecily onto her back. She lies naked in the grass as Mike D rips the condom from his shaft. He vigorously jacks himself off and chokes Cecily at the same time. His eyes roll back. "I'm going to cum. I'm going to cum on your fucking tits."

"Okay," Cecily squeals as Mike D's hot fluid trickles from her erect nipples to her navel. Her airflow is open again.

Mike D lies down next to stark Cecily. "You

are beautiful," he says, hugging her close.

Cecily closes her eyes as a single tear drops onto a blade of grass. She rubs her eyes and spots a patch of buttercups a few feet away. Water still plunges from the mountain just as it always has. "This is a beautiful place to be lost."

Now dusk, crickets chirp in the distance and fireflies glow as they drive home with the top still down. Mike D plays a song Cecily does not recognize and "Waltz of the Flowers" plays in her head. Costumed in tulle and lace, she gracefully pirouettes across the stage and bows before a full auditorium.

"Bravo!" her adoring audience cheers as bouquets of red roses fall to her slippered feet. The spotlight is hot and bright.

Mike E

"When was the last time you talked to Isabel?" Cecily asks, rummaging through her closet.

Liz applies rosy blush to her freckled cheeks in Cecily's dresser mirror and sticks a bobby pin into her tawny crimson hair. "I don't know, middle school, I guess." She sucks in her cheeks and applies more pink blush. "What about you?"

"We had French class together last semester. She let me copy her homework everyday but we never actually talked, well, except in French, but *je ne comprends* zilch." Cecily throws an embarrassing pair of unicorn printed pajamas across the room. "I'm surprised I passed that class at all, to be honest." She throws another pair of pajamas, pawprints this time, across the room. "We never spoke after that though. Not even *en Francais.*"

"Well, that was nice of her," Liz says, opening a bag of corn chips. "You want some?"

"No, thanks," Cecily says, holding a yellow mini skirt against her in the mirror.

"I haven't seen you eat in weeks, Cec."

"What are you talking about? We ate lunch together a few hours ago." Cecily shoves the skirt back into her closet.

"You nibbled on a turkey sandwich and then threw the bread away."

"Are you really paying that close attention to my sandwich as I eat it, Liz? You could have just asked for the leftovers. I would have been more than happy to share my turkey sandwich with my best friend."

"Don't be mean, Cecily." Liz exhales, chomping a corn chip. "I just care about you. That's all."

"I appreciate that, Liz, but I'm fine. I don't want any chips right now." Cecily continues to dig through the bottom of her closet.

Liz eats another chip. "So, that's the only interaction you've had with Isabel since—"

"Yeah," Cecily halts. "Since the disbanding of the Fearless Four. Since Flora left."

"The Fearless Four," Liz echoes. "Have you talked to Flora?"

"We used to write to each other almost every week when she first went away, but not so often anymore." Liz places her hairbrush into her duffel bag. "Her last letter came two months ago, and it was pretty out there, talking about phenomenology and *being*. I didn't really get it at the time. She really likes this French guy, Sartre, or she did two months ago anyway."

"Flora was always the most out there," Liz says. "Remember when she convinced us to sneak out of her house in the middle of the night to run through Mrs. Mitchell's garden?"

"Oh my god, yeah! That was the best. Remember Mrs. Mitchell the next morning?"

"*My prized lilies!*" they mock in unison.

"We barely even touched any of her stupid lilies. I think she was just bored or something," Cecily recalls. "But Flora's dad was so nice about it. Remember how he went out and bought her a dozen roses to apologize? And he wasn't even mad at us at all. He almost seemed proud of us or something."

Liz stares sullenly at a corn chip in her hand. "I miss her," she whispers.

"Me too," Cecily says. "I bet an all-girls

school is so boring though! Can you even imagine going to school without boys? I'd hang myself!" She tries on another sundress.

"It's a slumber party, Cec," Liz says. "Who cares what you wear?"

Cecily throws on an old yellow t-shirt. "I mean, I just don't get why Isabel invited us to this slumber party after dropping us like we were useless to her, and then ignoring us completely. She's popular now. She has a Brax Boy."

"I don't know, Cec. Maybe she misses us." Liz looks at her freckled face in the mirror again. "Or maybe she found out the most popular boy in school likes you. Your Brax cred is on the rise and you know how fast news travels in that school. I can't believe you haven't told me more about that date, by the way. You had sex with him, right?"

"I told you," Cecily says. "It was just whatever." She hangs her discarded clothing back up in her closet. "Sex doesn't really mean anything. It's just something to do, something we think we have to do. I thought it would be some special act of romance, but it's meaningless. You'll find out when you do it."

"Wow," Liz coughs. "You're *so* jaded and cool, Cecily. I can't wait to be as mature and enlightened as you someday. Maybe someday a living, breathing male will like poor old Liz someday."

"Liz, that's not what I meant at all and you know it!" Cecily shouts. "Don't make this all about you."

"Wow, you are one to talk, Cecily," Liz spits. "You are the most self-obsessed person I know."

"I'm sorry, I'm sorry. Can we please not fight?" Cecily begs. "I'm not trying to be condescending."

Liz stares at Cecily's bedroom floor. "Whatever."

"Mike D was nice. He had a very nice car,

he was very nice, but all in all it was just sex. Boring, even; nothing to write home about." Cecily looks at her Cocoa Bear peeking out from a pile of clothing in her closet. "I was naïve to think Mike A and I 'made love' or that he was 'The One.' That's all bullshit."

"Fine, okay, whatever. I don't want to talk about boys anymore, okay? I'm so tired of talking about boys," Liz moans. "Do you like this color?" she asks, extending her hands to Cecily. "It's called Herring Red."

Cecily's mom pokes her head through Cecily's bedroom door. "You girls ready?"

"Almost," Cecily says.

"There's a *Happy Days* marathon on tonight and I don't want to miss it." Cecily's mom enters the bedroom. "Are you excited for your Fearless Four reunion?"

"It's not really a reunion," Liz responds. "Flora won't be there."

"Even so," says Cecily's mom, "I'm sure you have a lot of catching up to do with Isabel."

"Let's just go," Cecily snaps, stuffing a nightie into her duffel bag.

"These Happy Days are yours and mine. Happy Days!" the television sings from the living room.

×

"Hi, girls! It's great to see you again!" Isabel's mother hugs Cecily and Liz. "Just like old times." She releases the girls from her embrace. "The other girls are downstairs. Do you remember the way?"

Liz smiles. "Of course. Do you need help with anything?"

"How sweet of you to ask!" Isabel's mother exclaims. "Would you mind bringing this tray of cookies downstairs? They're still warm."

"No problem!" Liz grins. "Did you bake

them yourself? They smell delicious!"

Vaguely annoyed, Cecily squints her eyes at her best friend. *Let's hope there are still some left by the time we get downstairs*, she thinks.

The two former Fearless Four members walk down the stairs to a place where they had played Would You Ever? and Truth or Dare; where they had eaten pizza and cookies without thinking about calories; where they had set their sleeping bags on the floor in a plus sign formation so they could talk until they could no longer keep their eyes open.

"*Bonjour*, bitches!" Isabel yells as she lights a candle. "You made it!"

The sound of Mike B's voice plays in Cecily's head. "*It's vanilla scented. Did you know vanilla is an aphrodisiac?*"

"Thanks for inviting us," Cecily says, dropping her duffel bag next to the pile of overnight bags on the floor. Liz finishes her second chocolate chip cookie and places the tray on a table alongside assorted chips and cans of soda.

"Girls, these are my friends, Cecily and Liz," Isabel says to the two other girls in the basement.

"Hey, I'm Jasmine." A slender olive-skinned girl with long, shiny black hair and black saucer eyes leans against a pile of ruffled throw pillows on the floor as she closely examines a fashion magazine.

Easily the most beautiful girl in West Braxton High, Jasmine, a junior, has always been beautiful, but her popularity is a recent development. Her wealthy grandfather had passed away a few months earlier, leaving her a small fortune. Jasmine's first purchase was a new nose. Taking a leave of absence to mourn, Jasmine recovered from her cosmetic surgery at a modest resort in Aspen. When she returned to Braxton County she bought a candy apple red Maserati.

"Another one with a snaggletooth! Calvin Klein always wants the bitches with the bad teeth. I don't get it." Jasmine angrily flips the page. "Nice to meet you."

"You too," Cecily says.

"I love your nail polish!" Liz says, stuffing another cookie into her mouth.

"Thanks!" Jasmine replies. "It's called Regal Rouge. *Rouge* is French for red but I think this is definitely more of a pink."

"Well, it looks really pretty on you," Liz coos.

"It's actually called Regal Rogue," Cecily chimes in, failing to mention that she had painted her nails the exact color last week. Liz didn't think the color was "really pretty" on Cecily, claiming that "Putrid Prostitute" would be a more fitting name for the shade. "Rogue is another word for dishonest tramp." Cecily stares at Liz. "But you're right, it's definitely more pink than it is red."

Jasmine returns her attention to her fashion magazine and sips on a bright pink beverage.

Stirring a large crystal bowl of bright pink punch, Isabel motions to a petite girl with a blonde ponytail discreetly smoking a cigarette out the window. "Hazel?" The blonde girl takes another long drag and puffs the smoke out the window. "Hazel!" Isabel shouts.

"Oh my god, what?" Exasperated, Hazel turns around, ashing her cigarette into a can of ginger ale.

Having dated every influential Brax Boy, Hazel, a senior, has been the most popular girl in West Braxton High since her freshman year. Defined by the silk ribbons she wears in her golden ponytail to match her cashmere cardigans, her emphatic voice and magnetic allure, Hazel is feared and admired. Hazel is completely prim, polished, put-together. She was accepted to all of her choice schools, but chose to take one year off, and take classes at the community college instead. New rumors are always spreading about Hazel–some true, some false–but Hazel always says, "There is no such thing as bad publicity." She does not deny nor confirm whether she tried to kill herself last summer.

"Say hello to my friends." Isabel demands. "And stop smoking cigarettes in here. It smells terrible."

"I'm working on my French inhale," Hazel rasps. "It's sexy, don't you think?" She contorts her face and attempts to inhale smoke through her nose.

"*Oui*," Cecily says wryly, still feeling weary of her situation.

"Hi, Hazel!" Liz chirps. "It helps if you pucker your lips like this." Liz adjusts her face to a freckly grimace.

Hazel mimics Liz and successfully inhales cigarette smoke through her nose. "Thanks for the tip, babe." She winks. "Liz, is it?"

"Yeah," Liz smirks proudly. "This is Cecily."

"Thanks for the introduction, Liz," Cecily says. "I would have forgotten my own name if it weren't for you."

"Tonight is going to be fun, I can tell already!" Isabel laughs coyly, walking away from the window.

"I didn't know you smoked," Cecily whispers to her best friend.

"It's not something I'm proud of," Liz replies defensively.

"I mean, I don't care if you smoke or not. It's your life." Cecily walks away from Liz.

"Do you girlies want some punch?" Isabel asks the two new girls, her old friends.

"Is there alcohol in it?" Cecily asks.

"Oh, yes," Isabel laughs. "There's alcohol in it. The guys at the liquor store think Jasmine is twenty-three."

"I don't look twenty-three," Jasmine adds. "I just have a fake ID."

"I'd love some punch," Liz says. "I'm not driving!"

"You don't have your license…" Cecily mumbles.

"No one is driving!" Isabel shouts. "My mom took everyone's keys. It's the only slumber party rule."

"So she knows we're drinking?" Cecily asks. "And she's fine with it?"

"My mom only has one rule, besides no drunk driving, and it's No Boys Allowed." Isabel ladles some punch. "She trusts us girls."

"Thanks, Izzy," Liz says, taking a glass of punch from Isabel.

Izzy? Cecily thinks to herself.

"Do you want some punch, Cecily?" Isabel asks.

"Cec has sworn on her own life to never drink again," Liz jokes.

"Thanks, Liz. I forgot I hired you as my

publicist." Cecily glares at her best friend. "I'm okay with water for now." Cecily scours the spread and cracks open a seltzer. "Chips, Liz? Aren't these your favorite?"

"I suppose I'll have another glass," Hazel breathes from the couch.

Ignoring Cecily's jab, Liz proudly presents her mighty Queen Hazel with a glass of pink punch. "Thank you, Lizzy." Hazel nods in approval.

Cecily chokes on her seltzer. *Lizzy? Am I dreaming?*

"Cheers!" Isabel enthuses, gathering her friends around the glass coffee table. "To Girls' Night!"

The girls clink their crystal glasses with Cecily's aluminum can. "To Girls' Night."

Hazel looks at the wall clock. "Mike E will be here in ten minutes. Jas, do you have the money?"

"Yeah, it's in the Louis." Jasmine points to her Louis Vuitton bag on the floor.

"Who's Mike E?" Cecily asks, leaning against

a purple plush cushion on the floor. "What about your mom's No Boys Allowed rule?"

"He's not coming inside," Isabel assures, "just to the window."

"What is he bringing here?" Cecily asks.

"Ecstasy, obviously." Hazel laughs. "Heard of it?"

"Yes, Hazel," Cecily says politely. "I've heard of Ecstasy."

"I detect an attitude…" Hazel bites.

"That's not an attitude. That's just her voice," Liz says, forcing a feeble laugh.

Cecily slams her seltzer onto the glass table. "Wow, Liz, you're so good at speaking for me, maybe you can take my French oral exam for me next week too."

"French oral exam," Jasmine repeats, still flipping through her magazine.

"Sounds hot," Hazel remarks.

Like a small miracle, a knock sounds at the

basement window. "He's here," Hazel snaps. "Give me the money." Grabbing three one hundred dollar bills from Jasmine, she sprints to the window. "Mikey, my fairy godfather. You're always on time."

"You girls getting wild tonight?" a hooded figure asks from the window.

"Not too wild!" Isabel laughs.

"Of course," Mike E says, taking the money from Hazel. "Pillow fights and pedicures, right?"

"You know it, Mikey," Hazel says, smiling for the first time all night. "Girl stuff."

"I'd love to be a fly on the wall for that," Mike E says as he hands Hazel the pills. "These are a little different from the last ones. Less speedy, no wicked comedown, very relaxing."

"Magnifique," Hazel says. "Thanks again, doll." She pecks Mike E on his shadowed check and closes the window.

"Let me see them!" Jasmine shrieks. "The

last ones had roses on them. What's on these?"

"Settle down, babe," Isabel says as Hazel drops six blue pills onto the glass table.

"Crowns," Jasmine states. "Chic."

"*Très chic*," Liz says.

"*Sacré bleu*," Cecily scoffs.

"Wow, your French is improving, Sizzle," Isabel smiles. "You probably don't even need to copy my notes anymore."

Sizzle?

Noticing Cecily's discomfort, Isabel hands her a pill. "I know you're not drinking, Cec, but are you okay with this?" she asks her old friend sincerely.

Cecily takes the pill and studies it in her hand. The engraving looks more like the letter E than a "crown" to her. "Girls just wanna have fun, right?" Cecily says before she pops the blue pill into her mouth.

"That's the spirit," Hazel says.

"To Girls' Night!" Liz shouts as the rest of the girls swallow their Ecstasy pills.

Isabel lights another candle on the glass coffee table the girls all surround it. The television is off but faint, nondescript music plays from the speakers. Cecily looks at her chipped nail polish, a striking shade of peach called Modern Marigold.

"Last time it took an hour to kick in," Jasmine says, still flipping through her magazine. "Oh my god, this girl is a cow!" She points to a model on the page. "Look!"

"Shut up, Jasmine," Hazel lightly reprimands, rolling her eyes.

"You shut up, whore!" Jasmine girlishly throws a pillow at Hazel.

Hazel giggles. "Not everyone can be naturally thin like you," she says and throws the pillow back. "That's all I'm saying. I'd kill for your body."

"You have the best tits on campus," Isabel says. "Everyone knows it."

"You'd know best, bitch!" Hazel throws an ice cube from her glass at Isabel. Isabel sucks on the ice cube. "Okay, what should we play?" she asks the girls.

"What about Would You Rather?" Liz suggests.

"Good idea, Lizzy," Isabel agrees. "That was Flora's favorite."

"You guys," Cecily interrupts with frustration, "Flora isn't here. Stop using her nicknames, *Izzy*, *Lizzy*, and *Sizzle*. Nobody calls me Sizzle except Flora, okay? The Fearless Four doesn't exist anymore, so stop pretending like it does."

"Chill out, Cec. They're just nicknames," Liz says as she sips her bright pink punch.

"It just sounds so forced, I'm sorry," Cecily sighs. "They're not just nicknames. They're Flora's nicknames."

"I'm sure Flor wouldn't mind," Isabel says firmly.

"Yeah, relax, Cec," Liz adds. "It's not a big deal."

"You know that's not true!" Cecily cries. "You too, Isabel!"

"Okay, Fearless Four, Shizzle Fizzle Brizzle, whatever you call yourselves," Hazel interjects with boredom, "you're acting more like the Three goddamn Stooges. Get it together."

"Who's Flora?" Jasmine asks, ladling more punch into her crystal glass.

"She was my—*our*—best friend," Cecily explains. "She goes to Everwood Prep now."

"Fancy little bitch, huh?" Hazel disparages.

"No," Cecily bites. "Her stepmother sent her there after her dad died in a car accident two years ago."

"An evil stepmother," Hazel laughs. *"Classique."* All the girls look at her in silence.

"Everwood is a really good school," Jasmine comforts. "She's probably doing all right–

learning Latin, probably."

Isabel lights another candle. "Let's just try to get along and have fun, okay?" She looks at Cecily and Cecily looks at the floor.

"Seriously," Hazel sighs. "Okay, what should we play? Would You Rather is clearly not an option." She looks at Cecily, who is still looking at the floor. "Cecily, honey, are you done with that seltzer?"

"Almost," Cecily says. "Why?"

"Let's play Spin the Bottle." Hazel smiles. "Or Spin the Can, rather."

"Spin the Bottle? With just girls?" Liz asks hesitantly.

"Yeah, why not?" Jasmine says, closing her fashion magazine.

Cecily finishes her seltzer. "What the hell." She sets the can on its side on the glass table.

"Isabel, it's your house," Hazel says. "You go first and then we'll go clockwise."

Isabel spins the can with effort. All six girls fix their eager gazes upon the can as it slows down before it stops and points to Jasmine.

"Come here, slut," Isabel says, reaching over to the beautiful black-haired beauty. They press their radiant rouge lips together and giggle.

"I guess I'm next," Cecily says shyly. The can spins gracefully and then points to Liz.

"There we go," Hazel coos. "Kiss and make up, girls."

Reaching over the table, Cecily pulls her best friend into a firm kiss. "Love you, bitch."

"Love you, too, Cec," Liz says earnestly as she hugs Cecily.

"Yes, we all love each other," Hazel says, utterly bored with the Fearless Four. "New rule: Before you spin, you have to remove an article of clothing."

"I like that rule!" Jasmine yelps, immediately taking her black halter top off. "My turn." The bottle spins and lands on Cecily. Cecily turns to Jasmine and wraps her arms around her bare chest as they kiss slowly and passionately.

"That was kind of hot," Jasmine says, peeling her lips from Cecily's.

Cecily opens her eyes. "Your lips are so soft," Cecily whispers. "I'm not gay but that felt nice."

"You sure, lesbo?" Hazel asks snottily. "It looked like you were about to cream yourself!"

"Shut up, Hazel!" Isabel yells as she hits Hazel hard on her arm.

"What?" Hazel snaps. "We're having a good time, right?"

"I'm not gay either," Jasmine says. "I just like kissing—and touching and feeling good. Girls have warm bodies too. They're not much different than boys." Intrigued, Cecily gives Jasmine her undivided attention.

"And boys never give you want you want," Jasmine continues. "When you're with a girl, you know what drives you wild and that same thing drives her wild too. Whatever you want, she wants it too. Boys don't care about that."

"Their brains turn off as soon as their dicks turn on," Isabel adds.

Cecily sits up. "They're all like that?" she asks, feeling a sense of relief. "Boys, I mean. Their brains turn off?"

"Not all of them," Liz says, playing with the empty seltzer can.

"Not all of them," Jasmine repeats. "But most of them, yes. They enter this crazy testosterone-driven world and they stop feeling compassion or something. They probably forget their own names." She sips her punch. "That's why I only hook up with college guys. They're experienced lovers."

"Do college guys think you're twenty-three, too?" Cecily asks.

"No, I tell them I'm eighteen," Jasmine says.

Bored, Hazel dips her index finger into a vanilla candle. "Isabel, Truth or Dare?"

"We're not playing Truth or Dare," Isabel says as she stirs ice cubes at the bottom of her glass. "Okay, truth," she relents, popping a cube into her mouth, chewing vigorously.

"Are you a lesbian?" Hazel asks.

Isabel swallows the ice cube. "Yes, I am a huge slut dyke!" Cecily and Liz exchange glances that mean "I knew it!" The basement is noticeably warmer, the candles glow brighter, and the girls' laughter is genuine. An uncontrollable grin smears across Cecily's face.

"Whose turn is it?" Jasmine asks.

"Mine!" Liz says, smiling from ear to ear. "New rule: Let's all remove two more articles of clothing."

"It *is* getting warm in here..." Cecily fans herself.

"*Hot,* even," Hazel beams. The girls strip down to their panties as the bass-heavy music now envelops the room like a pink vanilla cloud.

Pulling her vibrant red hair behind her back, Liz spins the seltzer can for what seems like ten minutes. Time stands still as the entire slumber party stares and grins. As the can spins in stop-motion frames, Jasmine grazes Cecily's thigh. Cecily sways and grins as she squeezes Jasmine's hand in her own. The room pulsates and undulates until the can lands on Isabel. Climbing across the table, Isabel pulls Liz onto the couch with her and they hold each other, kissing deeply, breathing heavily. A tangle of strawberry blond hair covers their soft, wet faces.

"Looks like Izzy and Lizzy are making the most of Girls' Night," Hazel says, though Cecily cannot hear her words. "You still feeling fearless?" Hazel asks Cecily. Unable to produce audible words, Cecily knows what Hazel wants, and she wants it too.

Complying with an unspoken agreement,

Cecily enters the fragile yet strong arms of Hazel. Their exposed breasts touch and Cecily is filled with warm, twinkling delight. Removing a hair tie from her delicate wrist, Hazel weaves Cecily's already matted hair into an effortless French braid.

"I never learned how to French braid," Cecily breathes, squirming slightly under the spell of Hazel's silken lips kissing her ribcage.

"Haven't you ever been to a slumber party?" Hazel whispers into Cecily's stomach. "It's something every girl should learn." Her eyelashes, thick with mascara, flutter across Cecily's torso. Cecily's body tingles as she strokes Hazel's smooth, petite frame.

"Lay down," Hazel playfully demands as she pushes Cecily onto her back, moving her small, blonde head lower and lower down Cecily's torso. Hazel's smooth pink tongue glides into Cecily. Cecily hoarsely moans as she wraps her legs around Hazel's frail neck.

"*Mon amie*, Jasmine." Hazel sits up and unties the red ribbon from her ponytail. "Do you want to French braid my hair, Jas? It's a slumber party tradition," she says enticingly, still massaging Cecily's breasts with her lithe French-manicured fingers.

In a shimmering pink daze, Jasmine drips hot candle wax onto her inner thighs and smiles. "*Oui, mon bichette*," she purrs, crawling behind Hazel. Jasmine combs her luscious blonde hair into a meticulous braid as Hazel simultaneously dives into Cecily with ease. Cecily grabs a maroon ruffled throw pillow from behind her as Hazel cups her warm mouth around Cecily's sensitive loins. Nibbling gently, Hazel caresses Cecily's throbbing clitoris with her experienced tongue, moving her head up and down, side to side, in dazzling circles. She looks to the couch to see Isabel and Liz thrusting into each other like bunnies. Cecily closes her eyes and visits a memory.

"Would you rather go to school naked for a day or eat Sizzle's mom's tuna casserole for a week straight?" Flora asks her friends. The Fearless Four lie atop their sleeping bags in Flora's screened-in patio. The air is sweet and moist, and Flora's father has just bade the girls good night.

"Naked, definitely!" Isabel giggles.

Flora laughs, "I agree, Izzy."

"It's not that bad," Liz says. "It's actually pretty good if you add enough ketchup."

"Lizzy, that is outrageous and disgusting," Flora says and turns to Cecily. "I'm sorry, but your mom's cooking is terrible, Sizzle."

"She tries!" Cecily yelps. "She's busy, you know. You're lucky your stepmom orders all of those meals in for you." Flora's bright face turns sullen. "You're right though," Cecily adds. "That tuna casserole is miserable."

"There are worse things, I suppose," Flora says. "My stepmother is a witch."

"She might be," Cecily says. "She seems to have your dad under some sort of love spell."

"Maybe she's just an incredible lover, if you know what I mean…" Isabel jokes.

"Shut up, Izzy!" Liz shouts, hitting Isabel with her pillow.

"Do you guys want to see Mrs. Mitchell's garden?" Flora proposes. "The sprinklers go off every night at exactly ten o'clock. It'll be so much fun!"

"I don't know if that's a good idea," Liz says. "Mrs. Mitchell is kind of scary."

"She's just an old widow!" Flora replies. "My stepmom—witch. Mrs. Mitchell—harmless."

"I'm in," Cecily corroborates as she sits up with excitement.

"I knew you would be, Sizzle." Liz smiles. "Come on, guys. Are we the Fearless Four or what?"

"We're the Fearless Four," Isabel says. "Come on, Lizzy. It's dark, no one will even see us."

"Fine," Liz says reluctantly. "But if we get in trouble, this was all your idea, Flora."

Flora creaks the patio door open as the Fearless Four shuffles outside. They sprint into the warm, dark night just as the sprinklers go off. The sweet sprinkler water saturates the roses, filling the air with a brilliant perfume. The ground is soft beneath Cecily's feet as she revels in the vivid aroma, waltzes in and out of the sprinklers with her beloved Fearless Four. She closes her eyes and listens to her best friends giggle and shriek with glee as she thinks, *This is the best night of my life.*

Passion rises in Isabel's basement as Cecily's body spasms with pleasure. "Oh god, yes!" She convulses as Hazel brings her to a hot, frenzied eruption. Panting loudly, Cecily's eyes roll back and her entire body is immersed in a fluid, tingling warmth. She releases a girlish roar.

Hazel rises from between Cecily's thighs as both girls steady their breathing. Jasmine is still behind Hazel, massaging her breast with one hand and pleasuring herself with the other. Jasmine climaxes and falls to the floor in Ecstasy. Hazel joins her atop an array of pink and purple ruffled throw pillows.

"Cecily," Hazel says, "come lie down with us." Cecily opens her eyes and the room is still moving, breathing almost. Her body feels the same hot confusion she felt when she spent that "enchanting" night with Mike A in the hot tub, right before she threw up. Trying to will the sensation away, she looks for Liz and Isabel, but they are no longer in the room. She joins her first female lovers on the floor. Their naked bodies melt into the basement floor as the room spins like the empty seltzer can for what seems like a year.

"Hey, sluts!" Isabel enters the room as Liz trails behind her, both with wet hair and wrapped in plush white towels. "Having fun staring at the ceiling?" Isabel jokes. Liz laughs like a hyena.

"I could always go for some more fun," Hazel says, covering her body with a cotton blanket. "Let's play a game."

"Another game, Haze?" Isabel says. "Was Spin the Can not enough for you?"

Hazel smirks. "Liz, Truth or Dare?"

"We're not playing Truth or Dare," Liz says, trying to snap out of her Ecstasy daze.

"Come on, it's Girls' Night." Hazel pouts.

But Liz resists. "I don't want to play."

"You scared?" Hazel forms a menacing grin. "I thought you were fearless…"

"She doesn't have to play if she doesn't want to," Isabel says, defending her precious Lizzy. "Let's watch a movie or something."

"It's just a game, Liz," Cecily murmurs, still swaying with the room. "I'll go next if you want."

"Fine!" Liz shouts. "Dare."

Hazel unweaves her French braid and ties her ribbon around her fresh ponytail. "I dare you to tell Cecily the truth about Mike A."

Cecily's hot, confused nausea abruptly returns as she jolts from her bed of throw pillows. "What did you just say?"

"Go on, Liz," Hazel says. "Tell your best friend the truth about you and Mike A."

"Am I dreaming?" Cecily stares at her best friend. "Liz, what is she talking about?"

"Cecily, I love you and I want you to know that," Liz begins.

"Oh my god, this is not happening. This cannot be happening." Cecily pierces Liz with a look of panicked agony. "Liz, just tell me!" she shouts.

"That pool party at Mike C's a few weeks ago..." Liz swallows. "The one you didn't invite me to—"

"The one Mike A exclusively asked me to be his date to? As his Plus One?" Cecily's body tingles with rage. "*That* party?"

"Yeah, that party." Liz says. "I saw you there. Don't you remember?"

"Are you kidding me? No, I do not remember seeing you there, Elizabeth." Cecily squints her eyes. "What the hell are you trying to tell me?

"Mike A was trying to carry you down the stairs. Your bathing suit was nearly off. I gave you water but you were too plastered to notice," Liz explains. "I helped Mike A situate you into Jared's car."

"This is all very confusing to me." Cecily cracks all ten of her knuckles. It's as if she can taste the sounds her joints make. "Why didn't you tell me you were there?"

"I was there earlier that evening." Liz says.

"A Brax Boy invited me, yes, *me,* to the same party, if you can even believe it. I had trouble following the directions on the map to the pool house and was lost in the woods."

"*Hopelessly* lost!" Hazel exclaims.

"Shut the fuck up, Hazel," Isabel snaps as she rubs Liz's back comfortingly.

"That's when I saw Mike A," Liz continues. "He helped me find my way to the poolhouse."

"And?" Cecily demands. "And then what happened?!"

"Well, we kind of hit it off. We talked about our families, our ambitions and dreams. The connection was so intense."

"Get to the point, Liz!" Cecily screams.

"One thing led to another and we made love in the hot tub," Liz says.

"No, Liz. A *series* of 'things' needs to happen before you're 'making love' in the hot tub with Mike A, the person who was there with *me.*"

"It just happened so fast, Cec. I felt terrible—we both did—so we agreed to pretend like it never happened." Liz swallows hard. "I was about to leave the party. I felt so guilty, Cec." She continues: "That's when you passed out in the sauna. Mike A didn't know what to do, so he asked for my help. We nursed you back to consciousness and got you a safe ride home. None of this was supposed to happen, Cec. I swear."

"You *made love*," Cecily dizzily barks. "This is unbelievable."

"We care about each other," Liz adds. "I really wanted to tell you. It broke my heart to hear you brood over him all the time."

"You could have just not done it! You could have stopped! You didn't have to fuck him fifteen minutes after meeting him, like a cheap whore."

"I know."

"And you could have stopped talking to him after it happened. Why would you pursue someone your best friend has been obsessed with for an entire year?"

"I know," Liz cries. "I know I could have done a lot of things differently, but I didn't. I'm so sorry."

"You could have told me," Cecily sobs. "I would have understood."

"You wouldn't have." Liz, also sobbing, sits down next to Cecily. "You were already too far gone. Every time I tried to tell you, you would insist that he was your one true love and that you would stop at nothing to be with him and a bunch of other psychotic shit. It's unhealthy to live in that fantasy world of yours where you and Mike A are together. It's not real."

"And what you have with him is real?"

"Yeah, we're in love." Liz rubs her eyes. "That's why we asked Mike D to take you out, to snap you back into reality. He's the hottest guy in school and he actually liked you, Cecily."

Speechless, Cecily stares at her best friend as tears begin to well in her eyes, ears and throat. Contempt rises and she wants to strangle her best friend until her face turns Languishing Lilac. Cecily attempts to clench her hands into fists but her body suffers from warm paralysis. "I would do anything for love," she says, "but I would *never* do that. You're my best friend."

"I'm sorry."

"My turn," Cecily whispers. "I choose Truth." She looks at her ex best friend's pathetic, backstabbing face. "Your mom thinks you're fat," she enunciates with satisfaction, "and I do too." She rests her head on a fuzzy magenta pillow. "You're a fat pig and I hate you."

"To Girls' Night!" Hazel toasts with the empty can.

"You're such a bitch, Hazel." Isabel barks. "Is this fun for you?"

"A little," Hazel says through her

laughter, "but it's better than sleeping on a bed of lies, *non?*"

Jasmine chimes in, "She has a point."

"Fuck all of you." Cecily pulls herself from the shag pile. "I'm going home."

"You can't! You're tripping on E!" Isabel cries. "My mom's not stupid. She'll ground me until graduation."

"Fine." Cecily gathers her belongings and climbs out the basement window. After stumbling in the darkness for an hour, Cecily finds a pay phone. She dials 1-800-GET-HOME.

×

"I thought Mrs. Mitchell would never leave," Flora's dad says to young Cecily and Flora as he pours fresh squeezed orange juice into tall glasses. The sun is bright and light speckles the spacious kitchen. There is no television in their kitchen and the birds chirp happily outside. "That woman sure can talk." He hands Cecily a cold glass of juice.

"I'm so sorry," Cecily says. "My mom should be here any second. She had a lot of appointments today."

"Stay as long as you want, Sizzle." Flora's dad smiles. "Think of this as your second home."

"Thank you," Cecily says graciously as she takes the glass of juice. She is aware that Flora's dad knows that Cecily has never met her own father. She assumes he is just being polite.

"I mean it," he says lovingly. "You are welcome here anytime."

Cecily sips her orange juice. "Thank you," she says, feeling warm and content. "I mean it," she says truthfully.

"We're really sorry, Dad," Flora says sincerely. "We didn't mean to violate private property."

Flora's dad laughs. "You know that isn't

true, Flor. That's why you snuck out in the middle of the night. You knew it was wrong, but you did it anyway."

"I guess so, yeah," Flora says. "It didn't feel wrong though."

"Did you have fun?" Flora's dad asks the girls.

"It was the most fun I've had in my entire life," Cecily says.

Flora nods in agreement. "Enchanting, even," she says with whimsy.

"Well, that's what counts in the long run," Flora's dad lectures. "Memories last a lot longer than lilies."

"Dad, we didn't touch her godforsaken lilies!" Flora protests. "I'm telling the truth!"

"She's right," Cecily adds. "We just ran through the sprinklers. No flowers were harmed in the process."

"I have a confession," Flora's dad says as he walks to the stainless steel refrigerator three times the size of the one in Cecily's home. "I picked these for you two." he hands Flora and Cecily two pristine lilies. "Don't tell the others, okay?"

Cecily takes in as much as she can of the moment because she wants to remember it forever.

×

"Thanks for the ride, Jared," Cecily says as he pulls into her driveway. "How much do I owe you?"

"Nothing." Jared smiles. "It's a free service."

"Are you sure?"

"Yes," Jared says. "Trust me, I know how easy it is to spiral out of control." He puts the car in park. "It's like you and your friends are on a beach and you're all digging a hole in the sand. You're having so much fun digging this hole that you don't want to stop. And no one else wants to stop either. Everyone wants to see how deep the hole can go. Eventually you get tired of digging and you're not having fun anymore. You look around at your friends and you wonder why you started digging in the first place. That's when you realize you're stuck in a very deep hole with no way out." Jared looks at Cecily. "Unless you have someone to help you out."

Silence washes over the car. "I never liked the beach," Cecily says.

"Me neither."

"Thank you, Jared." She adds, "Truly."

"No problem. Just know there's always a way out of any situation."

Still high on Ecstasy, Cecily tiptoes into her house. Her mother is passed out on the couch while the *Happy Days* theme song plays again. She covers her passed-out mother with a blanket and lies on the floor beside her. Watching the ceiling breathe above her, Cecily sinks into the sand.

"*It's ten o'clock,*" the television announces with foreboding. "*Do you know where your children are?*"

Mike F

Flora,

I hate her so much, Flora. I don't know what to do. I would do anything for Liz to feel what I'm feeling right now. It's so unfair. Everything is so unfair.

It's not even about Mike A, really. It's the fact that she thought I couldn't handle the Truth. She was right though. I can't.

I've allowed myself to exist in this world that doesn't exist at all. I don't like who I am, so I'm *trying to be someone else. It feels better to look in the mirror and not recognize myself. The Truth is ugly and I want nothing to do with it.*

Today was the last day of school. Everyone is going to the Fortress party tonight. It's this stupid tradition where all the popular kids camp out in some undisclosed location and burn their textbooks in a huge bonfire. You'd probably hate it. Anyway, I'm staying in. Going to one of those "traditional" Brax Boys gatherings is how all of this started. Plus, I wasn't invited.

My mom is selling Mrs. Mitchell's old house. The old girl is moving to Florida, I guess. Good for her, right? Her garden isn't the same; it's overgrown with weeds and all of her "precious lilies" are gone.

I know we used to tease Mrs. Mitchell when we were kids, but I always liked the way she took care of those flowers. She'd stay out there for hours every single day tending to them like they were her children. Maybe that garden was her way out, you know? I hope she gets a few house plants in Florida.

Anyway, there's an open house tomorrow. I don't have any other plans or friends, so I guess I'll go there with my mom. Maybe I'll bring Mrs. M some daffodils.

I'm sorry it's taken so long to respond to your last letter. Are you still into photography? The last photos you sent were beautiful. I hung the one of your shoes in the grass next to my bed.

I'm considering going to the Fortress party tonight just to ignore Liz. I want to ignore her so hard that it stings. I want her to feel so intensely ignored that it crushes her. I want her to feel ashamed to show the bruises left behind from the severity of my ignoring. I'm being dramatic, yes, but I'm so sad and alone. I trusted her, Flora. I don't trust anyone anymore. How can I? I trust you though. I hope you know you can trust me. I miss you so much.

Love always,

Sizzle

PS:You were right about Isabel! She's totally gay!

Without proofreading, Cecily carefully stuffs the thick cream colored stationery into a matching envelope, her monogram at the top right corner of both. This stationery set was a generous birthday gift from her aunt. Cecily considers writing her aunt a thank you note for the first time in fifteen years.

It's just paper, Cecily decides, and puts the box back on her shelf. She opens a jewelry box on her dresser and turns the key in the back. "Fur Elise" plays as a tiny plastic ballerina pirouettes. The jewelry box is also a gift from her aunt. *I'll write her tomorrow,* Cecily thinks.

Cecily walks to a small bookshelf in her room and pulls out a hardcover gold-leafed book of Brothers Grimm tales. As the plastic ballerina dances to a miniature piano, Cecily opens the book for the first time in two years. Pressed between two pages of *The Goose Girl* rests a flattened gray lily. Shed from their weak stem, brittle petals lie lifeless. The decomposed flower derides Cecily and the smiling lily that was once bright, soft, and fragrant. Cecily prefers the memory of her precious lily to the mockery of the sullen remnants lying between pages of lore.

Stricken with acute sorrow, Cecily realizes she is unable to mail a thank you note to Flora's father. She closes the book on another generous gift as the plastic ballerina's dance slows to a halt. She places the book back on the shelf and joins her mother in the living room.

"A temptress, or a device that produces a wailing warning sound," Alex Trebek answers.

"What is a siren?"

"Hey, Mom." Cecily sits on the floor and leans against the couch on which her tipsy mother lies.

"Hi, sweet pea." Cecily's mother smiles

as she strokes her daughter's hair. "Do you have big plans for you first night of summer vacation?" She lifts her head to sip a glass of vodka soda through a straw. "My baby girl made it through her first year of high school. Where does the time go? Just yesterday I was getting you ready for your first day of kindergarten." She takes another sip. "Do you remember?"

"Yeah," Cecily says, "I almost missed the bus."

"Because brushing your hair was like the Battle of Waterloo!" Cecily's mom says. "You refused to let me brush your hair. Every single morning you would scream and run away from me. I swear, Cecily Nicole, untangling that mane of yours gave me gray hair!"

"It hurt!" Cecily laughs. "But I liked the stories you used to tell me while you were doing it—Princess Pinky."

"Princess Pinky! That little girl with long, pink hair was always getting herself into trouble!" Cecily's mom laughs too. "I haven't thought about Princess Pinky in years. That was the only way you'd let me brush your hair! Once Princess Pinky was in the picture, getting you ready for school was a breeze."

"I know," Cecily says. "I wanted you to brush my hair all the time. I liked that she let little woodland creatures live in her hair."

"She was certainly fond of those animals, wasn't she?" Cecily's mother pets her daughter's head again. "And now look at you! My daughter is a blonde! Never did I think my baby girl would grow up to be a blonde bombshell." She strokes Cecily's hair. "We are getting so old."

"Yeah, I guess we are," Cecily says with a sigh.

"So, no plans tonight?" her mother asks.

"Nope. I thought we could hang out or something."

"Cecily Scott wants to hang out with her old bag of a mother on her first night of summer break? Is everything okay?"

"Yes, Mom!" Cecily assures. "Everything is fine. Calm down."

"Teens in Literature for a hundred, Alex," the contestant requests.

Cecily and her mother return their attention to Alex Trebek.

"She's sixteen at the beginning of Gone with the Wind, *and has a seventeen-inch waist, 'the smallest in three counties.'"*

"Who is Scarlet O'Hara!" The Scotts blurt out in unison.

"That's correct," Alex responds as the mother-daughter team high five.

"I'll take Ballet for 400," a TV contestant says.

"Before they were ballets," Alex Trebek answers, *"Copelia and* The Nutcracker *were 'Tales' of his."*

No one in the living room speaks.

"Who is Hoffman?" The contestant is correct.

"I'll take Mythology Books & Authors for 600."

"Answer:" Alex Trebek says, *"In an essay, Albert Camus compared the human condition to the myth of this rock pusher."*

"Who is Sisyphus?" Cecily utters.

"Correct."

"Wow! Nice one, sweetie!" Cecily's mother says, impressed.

"Math for 400."

"Like 4, this number is also the square root of 16." No contestants on the game show buzz.

"Negative four, obviously!" Cecily calls out.

"You're going to kick yourselves when you hear this," Alex Trebek tells his contestants. *"What is Negative 4?"* Unanimously confounded, the game show savants laugh.

"My beautiful blonde daughter is a genius, too!" Cecily's mother exclaims with pride, nearly spilling her drink.

"I took AP Calc this year," Cecily reminds

her mother. The Daily Double noise sounds.

"The category is Saints," Alex says to his lucky contestant. *"Until the twentieth century, this 'rower' was the only archangel with a feast day on the Western Calendar."*

Cecily feels a surge of inexplicable anxiety. "Who is Michael?" she murmurs hesitantly.

"Yes," Alex declares. *"Saint Michael is correct."*

Cecily's mother shakes the ice cubes in her nearly empty glass. "How did you know that? I never took you to church."

"I guessed," Cecily whispers. "Oh, Mom, look—" Cecily points to the television, "a real estate category. I bet you'll kill this." Cecily's mother pours more vodka into her glass.

"For one hundred dollars," Alex Trebek begins, *"real estate owned with no claims on it is said to be 'free' and this."*

"Free and clear!" Cecily's mother shouts, "What is clear?!"

"That is correct."

"Beauty and intelligence must be genetic!" Cecily congratulates her mom.

Cecily's mother shrugs. "That was an easy one."

Alex Trebek clears his throat. *"This term for the conveyance of property to secure a loan literally means 'dead pledge.'"*

"What is a mortgage?" Cecily's mom says with certainty, sipping her cocktail.

"As bleak as it is, 'mortgage' is correct," Alex Trebek smugly tells his contestants, the studio audience, and home viewers.

"You're on fire, Mom!" Eyes still glued to the TV, Cecily and her mother grin. As her mother weaves her fingers through her daughter's hair, Cecily takes note of this warm moment with her mother so she can save it forever. The phone rings.

"I'll get it," Cecily says, standing up from the floor.

"Thanks, sweet pea." Entranced and

intoxicated, Cecily's mother does not look away from the TV.

Cecily holds the phone receiver to her ear. "Scott Residence. This is Cecily."

"*Bon soir*, babe."

"…Isabel?" Cecily speculates, confused.

"No, honey. It's Hazel. Baby Belle gave me your number."

"How nice of *Baby Belle* to do so." Cecily wishes she could roll her eyes louder. "It's especially nice considering I haven't spoken to Baby Belle, or anyone for that matter, since her slumber party two weeks ago…"

"Relax, Cecily," Hazel coos. "Everyone has been *très* busy with term papers and exams and all that. Haven't you?"

"I guess so, yeah."

"Precisely," Hazel says, terminating the issue. "Anyway, you're coming to the Fortress party, right? I mean, obviously you're coming—

it's the biggest party of the year."

"Actually, I don't think so," Cecily says.

"Don't be preposterous, Cecily," Hazel asserts. "It's tradition—a celebration of summer freedom and a final farewell to our most honored senior Brax Boys. They throw this party every year for *us*. It's *très exclusif*."

"I don't really care for tradition," Cecily states, "or Brax Boys."

"Fuck tradition, then. Be spontaneous!" Hazel laughs. "It's summer, bitch. Let's have fun!"

Cecily looks at her mother on the couch. The bottle of vodka is nearly done and her eyes are glazed with inebriation. She'll be knocked out within the hour. "I don't know, Hazel," Cecily responds. "Why are you inviting me anyway? Why is it imperative that I attend the Fortress party? What does it matter to you?"

"Wow, Cecily," Hazel responds. "I'm only trying to be nice to you. I feel for you."

"You feel for me," Cecily repeats.

"Of course! I'm older than you. You think I haven't dealt with bitches and betrayal? I've had my share of bullshit, Cecily, and let me tell you— it's only going to get worse from here. You'll learn to keep your guard up to avoid it, but sometimes bitches need to be put in their place."

"I assume you're talking about Liz and Mike A," Cecily says.

"*Oui*, Captain Obvious. Aren't you upset? I would be furious if my best friend did that to me. She lied to you."

"Yeah, I'm not thrilled about the situation."

"And to set you up with another guy?" Hazel reminds Cecily. "Not only did she lie to you, she *pitied* you."

Cecily touches her neck and the taste of dirt returns to her mouth. She remembers how it feels to suffocate. Her body weakens. "Yeah."

"And to be pitied by a fat, freckly dyke!"

Hazel squeals. "Personally, I would have ripped the whore's frizzy hair out."

"She's not a dyke," Cecily says.

"Whatever, you're a fucking queen compared to that cow."

"I wouldn't go that far…"

"She's fat and you know it," Hazel concludes. "Anyway, I want to help you."

"How?"

"This bitch needs to be taught a lesson and you deserve your revenge," Hazel says, "and I believe revenge is a dish best served *à la mode*."

"Liz does like ice cream." Cecily laughs. "Fine, I'll go to the Fortress party."

"*Fantastique!*" Hazel exclaims. "See you in twenty minutes."

"You know where I live?"

"*Oui*, Baby Belle gave me your address. She feels terrible about your situation too, but Izzy and Lizzy have been joined at the fucking crotch lately."

"Weird."

"Girls are funny like that. You never know what to expect from them."

"Okay, I'll be outside in twenty minutes."

"Marvelous," Hazel says. "*Ciao*, bitch."

Cecily walks over to her mother and taps her on the shoulder. Final Jeopardy has just begun. "Mom, are you awake?" Cecily shakes her mother harder. "Mom!"

Startled, Cecily's mother opens her eyes. "What?"

"I'm going out with the girls," Cecily tells her. "I'll be home by ten." She intentionally leaves the bonfire part out; Cecily knows even the mention of the word "fire" triggers her mother.

"Oh, that's fine, honey," her mother says through her yawns. "You can stay out until midnight. You're a big girl now. I trust you."

"Wow, thanks, Mom," Cecily says gratefully. "I'll be home by then, don't worry."

"I never worry. The Scotts are fearless."

Cecily's mother feigns laughter before drifting back to sleep.

Cecily dresses herself in a pair of denim shorts and black tank top. Her denim shorts are now so loose they droop from her bony hips. Searching for a belt in her closet, she sees her Cocoa Bear. Cecily takes him out and hugs him close. She knows there is no room for him on her bed anymore. He may as well be pressed in her book of fairy tales.

A car honks from Cecily's driveway. In the passenger seat, Hazel works on her French inhale while Jasmine applies lip gloss in the mirror.

"I'm leaving, Mom," Cecily announces. "Are we still on for Mrs. Mitchell's open house tomorrow?"

"What?" Muddled, Cecily's mother murmurs, "Oh yes, the house. Tomorrow. Mrs. Mitchell. Have fun, sweet pea."

"I love you, Mom."

"Swing low, sweet chariot," Alex Trebek says, *"coming for to do this."* Cecily kisses her unconscious mother on the forehead.

"What is Carry Me Home?"

×

"Hey, slut!" Hazel shouts. "Happy first night of summer!"

"You, too," Cecily responds as she get into the back of the candy apple red Maserati. "Hey, Jasmine."

"Hey, Cecily," Jasmine says. "You live pretty far out here."

"Yeah, I know. Thanks for picking me up."

Jasmine turns the radio down as the car pulls out of the driveway. "How much do you hate Liz?" she says merrily over the lulled, incessant pop song.

"A decent amount, I suppose."

"Here's the plan." Hazel flicks her cigarette out the window. "You're going to get Liz to drink the Juice.

"What's the Juice?" Cecily asks. "And why?"

"It's some fucked up concoction that the Brax Boys use on party crashers," Hazel explains. "It's usually red. One sip and you're down for the count. The Boys usually strip their victims naked and paint them with West Braxton colors. They'll write 'I love dick' on their faces, or whatever. Harmless stuff, you know."

"And you want them to do that to Liz?" Cecily scoffs.

"Of course not, darling," Hazel continues. "They don't have to strip her or anything. Just get her to drink a few sips somehow and she won't know what hit her. You'll be able to take back what's yours."

"What's that? Mike A?"

"Duh! And people call me dense…"

"I don't think that's going to work, you guys. Liz isn't stupid," Cecily says. "I'm sure she knows to stay away from the Juice."

Hazel flicks her cigarette out the window. "Well, if that doesn't work, give her this." From her tiny pink coin purse she pulls out a blue pill and hands it to Cecily.

Cecily studies the small round pill in her hand. "What is this?"

"Rohypnol." Hazel lights another cigarette and exhales.

"I don't know, Hazel." Cecily looks at the pill. "How am I going to get Liz to take this?"

"Just talk to her like everything is cool. Tell her you want to smooth everything over, give her a hug and casually slip it in," Hazel proposes.

"Just fake it," Jasmine says. "She lied to you for months."

"So the plan is to roofie my best friend and then throw myself at her boyfriend, who wants nothing to do with me? He probably thinks I'm a nut job stalker too."

"Do you have any other ideas?" Hazel inhales *a la francais*.

"No." Cecily puts the pill in her back pocket.

"Do you want to be with Mike A or not?" Jasmine asks.

"I don't know what I want anymore."

"But you agree Liz needs to be punished for what she did, right?" Hazel says. "She humiliated you and everyone knows it." She pulls cigarette smoke deep into her lungs. "Look, I'm not going to force you to do anything. You can make your own decisions. I'm only trying to help."

"Thanks."

Jasmine pulls into a strip mall parking lot. Beyond the lot, there are heavy woods for miles. "We're here." As the girls exit the car, Cecily recognizes some of her classmates' cars parked in the lot, including Mike D's vintage convertible, which had once gotten her purposefully lost, and Jared's humble Toyota Corolla, in which she and Mike A had once shared an "enchanting" moment.

"Do you have the map, Jas?" Hazel asks. "I brought the compass."

"Yeah, it's right here." She unfolds a piece of paper and studies the hand drawn map. "It's far this year."

"Well, they probably don't want it busted like it was last year."

"True," Jasmine says, retrieving her backpack from the trunk.

"There's the first red flag." Hazel points to a red kerchief hanging from a tree. "We have to follow the red flags until we're there. According to the map, there are six. You girls ready?"

"I guess so," Cecily says.

"Let's get fucked up!" Jasmine exclaims as they enter the forest.

It is still bright outside but the thick trees

block the sunlight. Following the map, the girls reach the second red flag and take sixty steps east. They continue through the woods, checking in at each red flag. The final flag flies in the wind atop a steep hill as a cloud of smoke rises beyond it.

"I hope the Brax Boys have a water supply," Cecily says, out of breath. "I feel like I'm dying." Hazel and Jasmine laugh through their own exhaustion. "Why do they throw a bonfire party when it's a hundred degrees outside? And did they really need to hang six red flags? Seems like a lot of work for just a party."

"Tradition," Jasmine says as a bead of sweat drips down her chest.

"We're almost there," Hazel says, panting. "It will be worth it."

"I'm so hot," Cecily says.

"The bigger the hill, the bigger the plunge," Jasmine says.

"What does that even mean?" Cecily snaps.

"I don't know," Jasmine says. "It just came to me."

"Well, it doesn't make any fucking sense, Jasmine," Hazel whines.

"Sorry, I just said it! I don't know why!" Jasmine defends herself. "Maybe it would have sounded better in *French*."

"Let's just get to the top, bitches," Hazel demands as she tightens the purple ribbon in her golden ponytail. They strenuously climb their way to the final red flag in silence.

Dripping with sweat, the girls reach the top of the hill. Cecily holds onto a tree branch for support. Though grateful she wore sneakers, she wishes she had eaten the macaroni and cheese her mother left out for her.

"Finally!" Jasmine cries. They look out from the hill and see the Fortress. There are no flowers or waterfalls in the barren field miles away from town. A couple dozen tents surround a bonfire, and one large tent sits a few yards away from the rest of the Fortress. Cecily knows that is the beer tent. Brax Boys think they are clever, but they are so predictable, she thinks, as she decides whether she'll drink tonight or not. After all, it is the first night of summer and her curfew is extended to midnight.

"Shit, I forgot to bring books to burn," Hazel says.

"You can borrow some of mine, Haze," Jasmine offers. "Cecily, did you bring anything to burn?"

In a crowd of her peers, Cecily spots Liz's frizzy red hair; she's standing next to Mike A. She touches the scepter pill in her back pocket. "Just bridges." Hazel, Jasmine, and Cecily carefully plod down the hill to join the wildest, most exclusive and fun party of the year.

"Welcome to the Fortress!" a Brax Boy

exclaims as he nonchalantly tosses a western civilization textbook into the growing bonfire. "Help yourselves, ladies. The beer tent is stocked."

There are twice as many people at the Fortress party as there were at Mike C's pool party. Cecily does not recognize the faces of most of the people and wonders if they even attend West Braxton High. The trees above the Fortress block out the rays of the sun and the bonfire illuminates the temporary teenage village a dull vermillion. Defining features of everyone's faces are masked with the hazy sepia glow emanating from the books ablaze. Every temporary Fortress resident, Brax alum or not, is indistinguishable and unfamiliar.

Several Brax Boys flock to Jasmine, who is wearing a form-fitting sparkly blue dress with a plunging neckline. Even amidst the obscurity of smoke, Jasmine's beauty radiates. She is stunning when she does not speak: the perfect girl for any Brax Boy. Jasmine accepts a key bump of cocaine from a lanky Brax Boy and laughs coyly. She grabs the Brax Boy's wrist and guides another key of powder to her nose.

"Hazel, you want some?" Jasmine shoves the Brax Boy's wrist in front of Hazel's face.

"You know it, bitch." Hazel, wearing a lacy purple cardigan to match her purple hair ribbon, smiles as she inhales the powder. "Cecily? You want?"

"No, thanks," Cecily responds politely. "I'm going to check the beer tent for water and maybe some spare books to burn."

Cecily departs from the cocaine circle and walks over to the beer tent. She is grateful no one makes an effort to speak to her. Detouring around people rabidly ripping pages from their history books and smashing beer cans on their heads, she steps into the beer tent, which is a large tarp supported by upright logs. She thinks of all the effort that went into creating this

Fortress and feels a twinge of embarrassment and sadness. She walks to a cooler and pulls out a can of seltzer. The cold can brings her back to Isabel's slumber party and Cecily feels sick again. She pours the seltzer into a red plastic cup and tries not to gag on the memory of Spin the Can.

"Still not drinking?" Cecily's stomach drops as she hears the most recognizable voice she knows. Liz, wearing Mike A's worn baseball cap on her frizzy head, stands before her. "I thought you'd give in by now, after swearing on my life and all. I know I would."

"What is that supposed to mean?" Cecily barks. "And why are talking to me?"

"I don't know why I said it that way." Liz stumbles over her words. "I meant, I'm a bad friend and you shouldn't care what happens to me. Or, have a drink–it's summer."

"Is that supposed to be some kind of apology?

Or are you trying to humiliate me even more?" Cecily tightens the grip on her cup of sparkling water. "I can't believe you're talking to me right now, Liz. Did someone drug you or something?"

"I just wanted to tell you not to drink the red jungle juice," Liz advises her former best friend. "That's what the Brax Boys give to the party crashers. It'll make you puke until you wish you were never born."

"Wow! That sounds remarkably similar to how I feel talking to you right now, Liz." Cecily remembers the pill in her back pocket. Now is her chance to slip it into her seltzer and offer it to Liz. "And to come up to me while you're wearing that hat…"

"I'm only trying to help," Liz says. "I'm sorry, Cecily."

"So am I." Cecily takes the pill from her pocket as she sips her non-alcoholic beverage. As she is about to drop it into her cup, a whirring explosion crackles from outside the beer tent. The pill falls to the ground as everyone runs out of the tent to see what happened. Cecily picks up the roofie and scurries out as well.

"You can't light fireworks out here!" A Brax Boy yells, "Are you trying to get us all killed? Do you want the cops to bust the Fortress before midnight?"

"Juice him!" Another Brax Boy throws a geography book into the fire. "Teach him a lesson!"

"It won't happen again," the guilty partygoer says as he throws the rest of the fireworks into the woods. "It was a small one anyway. Kid stuff."

"JUICE HIM, JUICE HIM, JUICE HIM, JUICE HIM," Brax Boys chant as the faceless fire-starter cowers in fear.

"Like a bonfire in the middle of the woods is safe to begin with," Mike A says. "He knows what he did. He doesn't need to be juiced. Let's just have a good time, okay?"

Cecily considers juicing herself when she hears Mike A's shrill voice of reason over the Brax Boys' chant, while fat Liz holds onto his arm for safety from the big bad fireworks. *King and Fat Queen of the Fortress*, she thinks as she fantasizes about starting a revolt with the fireworks boy.

"Thank you." The frightened culprit bows before his smug king, Mike A. Liz hugs her boyfriend proudly and Cecily sweats with nausea and fury. *I still can't believe this is real*, she thinks.

Walking away from her traitor best friend and Mike A, Cecily searches for a distraction. She heads toward the pile of used books. Mike C, drenched in sweat but jolly as ever, sorts through the academic kindling. Cecily imagines he would much rather be in his pool. He hands Cecily a book. "Happy first night of summer, freshman."

"Actually, I'm not a freshman anymore." Cecily takes the book from Mike C and laughs. "Do you seriously want me to burn *Fahrenheit 451*?"

"Pretty funny, right?" Mike C says, ripping the pages out of an SAT prep book. "All you need is *Cliffs Notes* anyway. Let it burn, baby!"

"You can do the honors." Cecily hands the novel back to Mike C. "Happy Fortress party!"

Bradbury's obsolete work strengthens the Fortress fire as Cecily scampers through the hot brume of ash and intoxicated teenagers. Squinting her eyes in pursuit of entertainment, or at least a distraction, she wanders to the other side of the Fortress. She returns to the circle surrounding Jasmine, who's now dressed in nothing but her bra and panties. A Brax Boy waves her sparkly blue dress above his head, playfully threatening to throw it into the fire to create "stardust."

"Jasmine, I think you've had enough

'stardust' for a while," Cecily asserts. "And that dress looks expensive."

"I have three more!" Wildly flailing her body like a deranged ostrich, Jasmine attempts a maladroit pirouette. "It's so hot. I can't breathe!"

"Have some water." Cecily hands Jasmine her cup of undrugged seltzer and turns to the Brax Boy holding the shimmering designer dress. "Can you please give Jasmine her dress back? I can assure you it will not produce stardust, just very expensive fumes." The Brax Boy courteously gives Jasmine her dress back. As Jasmine chugs the rest of Cecily's water, she throws the dress into the bonfire anyway. The Brax Boys cheer and Cecily walks away without her empty cup. Stardust does not appear.

Still unable to partake in the ceremonious book burning, Cecily sits on a log beside the Fortress fire. Waves of heat lick her face and smoke stings her eyes, choking her slightly. Still sober, Cecily revels in this fleeting moment of serenity.

Cecily's brief moment of zen is shattered as a breeze clears the smoke from her eyes. Across the bonfire she sees Liz and Mike A huddled together on a log. They are not kissing or even touching, but they are genuinely laughing. Cecily's heart sinks and she pulls the Rohypnol pill out from her back pocket. Examining the pill, a precise deep voice bellows abreast of her.

"Life's like that, you know?" Mike D pulls a drag from his tightly rolled joint. "It's all a roll of the dice."

Though enveloped with the heat of the Fortress fire, Cecily shivers. "Excuse me?"

Mike D holds smoke in his lungs and nods his head toward Liz and Mike A. "I know that must hurt," he says as he exhales, "but you can't let it bring you down. You have to let things go.

Trust me."

"I don't use the term 'trust' lightly anymore, but you have a point." She stands up from the log. "Thank you, and best of luck to you in New York."

Cecily floats away from Mike D without asking about the circumstances behind their escapist date, or why he called her a slut while he suffocated her. Even if she knew, it would not make a difference. It still happened. She throws the pill into the pit of flames.

Acting upon her moment of clarity and the pseudo-wisdom shared by Mike D, Cecily decides to confront her ex best friend and the boy she had once considered The One. She is ready to let go.

"Hey," Cecily says shyly as she approaches the happy couple. Liz and Mike A exit their tiny world of teenage love and look up at Cecily in silence.

"I just wanted to say hello," Cecily reiterates.

"Hello, Cecily Scott," Mike A says as Cecily tries not to crumble like a burnt textbook. "Are you enjoying your first Fortress party?"

"It's okay, I guess," Cecily responds. "It's so hot. I'd rather be at a pool party. I'm sure you two would agree." Liz and Mike A say nothing. "I'm kidding!" Cecily proclaims with laughter. "Too soon for jokes, perhaps."

"Perhaps…" Liz echoes.

"Anyway," Cecily continues, "I just want to tell you that I have no sore feelings toward either of you." She kneels beside Liz. "I want you to be happy, Liz. You're my best friend."

"Thanks, Cec," Liz says. "That means a lot. I want you to be happy too." Cecily hugs Liz. "Are you drunk?" Liz asks.

"No!" Cecily exclaims. "I just learned that I need to let things go. Life keeps going, no matter what. Dwelling in the past or in some kind of fantasy world is futile."

"Futile," Liz repeats.

"Cecily Scott, have you been smoking Mike D's grass?" Mike A jokes.

"No, I have not," Cecily states firmly, "and yeah, it hurts to see you guys together—it hurts a lot—so I'll probably need my space for a little while. I hope you can understand, Liz."

"I understand completely, Cec," Liz says. "We both do."

Cecily tries to ignore the sickness in her stomach elicited by the term "we." She looks at Liz and Mike A and then looks around the Fortress party. Her peers shout and run rampant as they toss their schoolbooks into the enormous fire. Everyone is covered in sweat and ash. "Do you have the time?" she asks Mike A.

"It is half past ten, Cecily Scott," Mike A says matter-of-factly. "Shouldn't you be turning into a pumpkin soon?" It amuses Cecily to see

Liz shift nervously on the log.

"My mom extended my curfew to midnight." Cecily smiles.

"Like a proper princess." Mike A smiles back.

"That was nice of her," Liz interrupts. "I heard she's selling Mrs. Mitchell's house. So weird—she's been there forever and we have so many memories of her garden."

"Yeah, it's pretty weird," Cecily says. "She's old though. Old people love Florida." They all laugh half-heartedly. "And besides, memories last longer than lilies."

"What?" Liz asks, puzzled.

"Never mind," Cecily says, looking around the Fortress. "I think I'm going to head home anyway. It's so hot. I don't think I can stand it much longer."

"I don't blame you," Mike A agrees. "Luckily Lizzy and I set our camp up far away from the fire."

"How excellent!" Cecily sneers, trying to hide her grimace. "Lizzy, your mom is letting you spend the night in the middle of the woods with a bunch of book-burning drunk teenagers?"

Liz shifts on the log again. "She thinks I'm at your house."

Cecily laughs. "Of course she does." She hugs Liz again. "Don't worry, I'll cover for you if she calls," Cecily says earnestly. "I should get going, though."

"Do you have a ride?" Mike A asks. Cecily looks for Jasmine, who is now topless and laughing maniacally in the grass.

"Actually, I don't," Cecily admits. "I saw a payphone in the parking lot. I can just call a taxi."

"Don't be ridiculous," Mike A insists. "Jared is on call again tonight. He should be in the parking lot right now."

"Wow, Jared is a really good friend to always be the designated driver for these gatherings,"

Cecily says.

"He doesn't mind," Mike A assures her. "I think he likes feeling needed."

"Who doesn't?" Cecily says. "Thanks a ton. I will give him your well wishes when I see him."

"Wait, Cec. Take this." Liz opens her bag and pulls out a flashlight. "I'm not leaving until morning, so I don't need it. You remember the way back, right?"

"Yes, I climb the huge hill and look for the six little rags hanging from the trees."

"Yeah, the hill is the hardest part," Mike A says. "After that, it's a piece of cake."

"Easy as pie." Cecily stops herself from making a pie joke at Liz's expense. "Thanks for the flashlight and the ride recommendation." She curtseys before the young lovers. "Happy first night of summer!"

Flashlight in hand, Cecily makes her way to the edge of the Fortress without saying goodbye to anyone. She feels content with the interactions she had with her peers, and anyway, everyone is too drunk to notice.

Cecily reaches the steep hill and laughs to herself about Jasmine's "the bigger the hill, the bigger the plummet" comment. She takes a deep breath and begins to climb. Moments later she is at the top. She looks down at the Fortress ablaze with a crimson glow. A Brax Boy throws the tarp from the beer tent onto the bonfire. She bids the Fortress farewell and navigates her way down the treacherous hill as she thinks of the letter she will write to Flora when she gets home.

Finally reaching the bottom of the hill, Cecily shines her flashlight around the woods in search of a red flag. It is pitch black and still. Cecily is hyper-aware of the eerie stillness and reminds herself she is almost out. She spots the second red flag and paces toward it as quickly as her clumsy feet can carry her. Reaching the flag, she sees the rest of the flags, as they are only a few yards apart. She is grateful the Brax Boys lack the capacity to create a clever map, putting most of their effort into book burning.

Nearing the next red flag, Cecily sees the faint fluorescent glow of the strip mall parking lot when she is knocked to the ground with force. Doubled over, she hears rustling in the bushes around her and frantically reaches for the flashlight on the ground beside her. She hears more rustling and heavy clambering. "Hello?" she sputters, trying to be brave. "Is someone there?" As she inches her hand toward Liz's flashlight, it is kicked away from her.

"What do we have here?" a shrill voice taunts as he picks up the flashlight. "Looks like some West Braxton trash," another voice says.

The shrill voice looms over Cecily. "Mike F hates to see trash on his property. You know this is private property, right?"

Cecily coughs. "I—"

"How dare you speak to Mike F!" the second voice boasts. A boot kicks Cecily in the ribs. "Can you believe the nerve of this one?"

"Not surprised," Mike F says to his accomplice. "Entitled Braxton scum." He kicks Cecily onto her back and shines the flashlight into her face. "Fucking maggot. Your Brax fags can't help you now. You're on my property." He spits in her face. "You belong to me." Mike F flashes the light away from Cecily's face. "Pick it up," he says to his accomplice.

"What do you want me to do with it?"

"We're going to teach it a lesson," Mike F sneers. "Trespassing is a crime."

The two faceless bodies kick Cecily's weak body down a hill and drag her into a pile of sharp rocks. She tries to cough but cannot. "Please don't hurt me," she begs but no sound leaves her mouth.

Mike F shines the light into Cecily's face again. "I'll tell you what," he reasons, "if you can get up and run away from me, I won't stop you."

"You're gonna let it get away?" the accomplice barks. "Just like that?"

Mike F ignores his accomplice and leans closer to Cecily. "You think you can run?"

Paralyzed with fear, Cecily stares into the light.

"What's the matter?" Mike F clobbers her on the side of the head with the flashlight. "No fight in you?"

Cecily remains on the ground.

"Too easy," the accomplice howls. "Too fucking easy."

"Fucking useless maggot." Mike F rips Cecily's denim shorts and panties to her ankles. "Tie it up," he barks to his accomplice.

While his accomplice secures her arms around a tree stump with a red flag, Mike F mounts Cecily, pinning her down with his knees.

"Open your fucking mouth." He pries her jaw open with his hand and hocks phlegm into her mouth. "Fucking parasite." Mike F slaps Cecily and shines the flashlight in her face. "Why aren't you resisting?" He unbuckles his belt and forces himself into near-comatose Cecily. "Fight me, maggot!" He shoves the weapon into Cecily as tears stream down her cheeks.

"Put your cock in it," Mike F grunts to his accomplice. "Down its throat."

As Mike F penetrates Cecily with the cold metal flashlight, the accomplice climbs over Cecily and straddles her face with his strong legs. "Suck my cock," the accomplice says, suffocating her with his fleshy dagger.

Cecily closes her eyes.

"I'm going to be late for the ball!" Princess Cecily cries beneath a luscious plum tree in the center of an intricate labyrinth. "I have been stuck in this bewitched labyrinth for hours.

Whatever will I do?" She looks around the enchanted maze and shouts for help. "Where is my prince? My carriage will surely leave without me if I cannot find my way out." Princess Cecily helplessly sobs into her elegant hands. "I will never live happily ever after if my charming prince does not rescue me! Where could he be?"

"He's not coming, Princess," a powerful voice echoes.

"Who is that?" Princess Cecily cries. "Do I know you?"

"I hope so!" another voice shouts.

"Show yourselves!" Cecily demands as the plum tree above her bursts into flames. Through the purple smoke three familiar figures appear before her.

"Long time no see, PC." Princess Flora leads Princess Liz and Princess Isabel through the hot debris.

"Princesses!" Princess Cecily hugs her

estranged royal companions. "It's been ages!" The four princesses embrace as another tree catches fire. "I'm so happy to see you all again! It's just like old times. Have you girls come to rescue me?"

"Not quite," Princess Flora coughs.

"What do you mean?" asks Princess Cecily.

"She means we're all stuck in here," Princess Liz interrupts. "And there's no way out."

"There's always a way out," Princess Cecily asserts. "There has to be." Blue flames explode in the air. "It's getting stronger," says Princess Liz.

"What's getting stronger?" asks Princess Cecily.

"The Hooded Monster," Princess Liz interjects.

"Is that what put us in the labyrinth?" asks Princess Cecily. "The Hooded Monster?"

"No," Princess Flora explains. "I'm not sure how we all ended up here but the Hooded Monster is responsible for setting the labyrinth ablaze."

"And it's getting bigger!" Princess Isabel cries. "We have to move fast."

"What are we supposed to do?" Princess Cecily cries. "We're helpless princesses."

"Get a grip, PC," Princess Liz sneers. "We're not helpless."

"We're a team," Princess Isabel says with confidence. "We're the Fearless Four."

"We must fight," Princess Flora orders, "if you want to make it to your ball alive."

"Fight with what?!" cries Princess Cecily as a flaming branch pierces through the labyrinth wall.

"With what we have." Princess Flora assesses a map and scours the perimeter. "All we have is this red juice, a flashlight, some red flags, and a map," says Princess Liz.

"And these." Princess Flora holds out a bouquet of lilies. "Here's the plan." Princess Flora begins. "Liz, hold onto this." She gives Liz the map and turns to Isabel. "Isabel, you're going to distract the Hooded Monster with these." She hands Isabel the bouquet. "They have sedative properties and no monster can resist them. The Hooded Monster will be knocked unconscious for approximately five minutes." Flora pauses as several trees explode around them. "That's when we make our move!" she shouts over the commotion.

"What if the monster wakes up before we find our way out?" Cecily shouts.

Princess Liz gives Princess Cecily the metal flashlight. "You'll have to kill it with this."

"How am I supposed to—" Princess Cecily is cut off by a circle of flames trapping the Fearless Four. An upright scaled beast towers over them twenty feet in the air. The monster has no face but a long, powerful tail on which spikes protrude.

"There is no escape!" roars the monstrous beast. "You will never defeat me!"

"Isabel, now!"

Isabel steps toward the Hooded Monster and waves the bouquet around as poison wafts from the silky petals. The Hooded Monster weakens and slowly falls to the ground, nearly crushing the fearless heroines.

"Juice it!" Liz commands as she throws the red flags and juice to the princesses. Liz and Isabel study the map while Cecily and Flora tag team the monster. They lift the hood from the beast to reveal two small black eyes and a sliver of a mouth. Flora pries the beast's mouth open while Cecily pours the red juice down its throat before gagging it with the red flags. The Hooded Monster is knocked out.

"We don't have much time," Flora yells. "That beast won't be down for long. We need to find the way out."

Princess Liz stuffs the map into her corset. "This way!" Leaving the Hooded Monster behind, the Fearless Four run through the burning maze.

"I can see the exit!" Princess Isabel exclaims. "We're so close!"

Princess Cecily peers through the burning vines and spots her royal carriage in the distance. She can practically taste salvation on her lips when she is knocked to the ground and separated from the other princesses.

"There is no escape!" The Hooded Monster cackles. "You will never get out alive!" The monster charges at Princess Cecily but she does not flinch. Ready to fight, she grips her flashlight as it becomes a sword. The Hooded Monster pounces at Fearless Cecily as she dodges out of the way. The monster rears up at her once more, nearly crushing her against a blazing peach tree. With a newfound superhuman strength Cecily pummels the beast, pinning it to the ground. "There's always a way out," says Fearless

Cecily. She stabs the monster in the heart. Cecily pulls the sword from her slain victim as dark green blood spurts from its chest. The fiery labyrinth turns to ash. Fearless Cecily marches triumphantly toward her royal carriage.

"We did it," Fearless Cecily says to the other heroines. "We made it out alive."

"We did it together," Liz replies.

"I never doubted you." Cocoa Bear hugs Fearless Cecily. "You've always had the means to escape. It's been within you all along." Cecily joins the rest of the Fearless Four in the carriage as the royal coachbear readies the reigns. "To the ball, Princess?"

"I think I'm done with balls for a little while, Cocoa." She exhales. "Let's go home." The royal carriage soars into the pink and orange sky.

Still secured to the tree stump, Cecily slowly opens her eyes to find herself alone with Liz's flashlight beside her. What a kind gesture for

Mike F and his accomplice to leave her with such a gift. Her body feels malleable and soft, as she is able to slip her wrists out from the makeshift harness with ease. She touches her warm head to see if she is bleeding. She is grateful that she is not, but she is covered in warm liquid just the same. Picking up the flashlight, Cecily searches for her discarded clothing. Unable to find her underwear, Cecily slides her denim shorts over her aching body. She walks back to the path of red flags created by the Brax Boys.

As she sees the last red flag before the parking lot, she feels compelled to run, or perhaps cry, but she continues with a steady trudge. Cecily walks to the most beautiful fluorescent lights she has ever seen in her life, exhaling as her feet touch the glistening pavement of the strip mall parking lot.

A car flashes its headlights, nearly blinding Cecily. She covers her eyes and waves and continues her elegant trudge toward the familiar chariot. She opens the passenger door and sits down. In the driver's seat, Jared reads a newspaper and sips a can of soda. "Cecily, are you okay? What happened to you?"

"Just another crazy Fortress party." Cecily laughs.

"Do you want a ride?"

Cecily nods, "Yes, Jared. I would love a ride."

"Your wish is my command," Jared says with a smile. "Are you sure you're all right? Are you thirsty? Do you want some seltzer? I have a twelve pack in the back."

"No, thank you, Jared," Cecily says, looking at the clock on the dashboard. "I need to be home by midnight."

"Like a real princess," Jared responds. Cecily rolls the window down and lets the summer air weave through her fingers until she is home.

ABOUT THE AUTHOR

Al Bedell is a writer who splits her time
between New York and Los Angeles.
She studied philosophy at the University of
Hartford. This is her first work of erotica.

I Would Do Anything For Love
is available as an enhanced ebook
with additional multimedia content for
Apple iBooks and Amazon Kindle.

For more information, visit
www.badlandsunlimited.com